But she had. The fact that she was sitting with Cal bore testimony to that. Sad part aside, she was loving every minute of it.

Looking at Cal, her eyes soaked him up like a sponge, taking in the way his clothes emphasized every muscle they covered. For a mad moment she envisioned him naked.

She sucked in her breath and held it. She had to stop thinking like that.

Suddenly she felt Cal's gaze on her, giving her a decidedly sensual appraisal. But it was when his eyes narrowed and dropped to her mouth that a flame ignited in the depths of her stomach.

She shouldn't care what he thought or how he reacted. But she did, and that was what bothered her. This man had managed to slip under her skin and touch her in a way no other ever had.

Dear Reader,

Books have always been part of my life. I've read them, sold them and written them. After graduating from college, I became a librarian, then I became a bookstore owner, then I became a romance writer. As you can see, every career I've had has dealt with books. How much better than that can it get?

Since I closed my bookstore several years ago, I have devoted all my time to writing and reading. I work in an office away from my home. I arrive around six-thirty each morning, and begin my workday. I love an office atmosphere as I have nothing to distract me from writing my stories. There I dream up lots of plots that, hopefully, readers will enjoy.

As well as my other books, I hope you will enjoy reading this one as much as I enjoyed writing it.

Happy reading!

Mary Lynn Baxter

MARY LYNN BAXTER

To Claim
His Own

Published by Silhouette Books
America's Publisher of Contemporary Romance

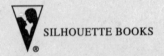 SILHOUETTE BOOKS

ISBN-13: 978-0-373-76740-3
ISBN-10:   0-373-76740-4

TO CLAIM HIS OWN

Copyright © 2006 by Mary Lynn Baxter

This edition published by arrangement with Harlequin Books S.A.

® and TM are trademarks of Harlequin Books S.A., used under license.
Trademarks indicated with ® are registered in the United States Patent
and Trademark Office, the Canadian Trade Marks Office and in other
countries.

Visit Silhouette Books at www.eHarlequin.com

Printed in U.S.A.

Books by Mary Lynn Baxter

Silhouette Desire

Mike's Baby #781
Dancler's Woman #822
Saddle Up #991
Tight-Fittin' Jeans #1057
Slow-Talkin' Texan #1177
Heart of Texas #1246
Her Perfect Man #1328
*The Millionaire Comes
   Home* #1387
Totally Texan #1713
To Claim His Own #1740

MARY LYNN BAXTER

A native Texan, Mary Lynn Baxter knew instinctively that books would occupy an important part of her life. Always an avid reader, she became a school librarian, then a bookstore owner, before writing her first novel.

Now Mary Lynn Baxter is an award-winning author who has written more than thirty novels, many of which have appeared on the *USA TODAY* list.

You can contact Mary Lynn by e-mail through her Web site, www.MaryLynnBaxter.com

One

Calhoun Webster's mouth fell open, then he slammed it shut.

His attorney and friend, Hammond Kyle, gave a semblance of a smile. "It's easy to understand why you're speechless. Under the same circumstances, I'm sure I would be, too."

"Are you jerking my chain, Kyle?" Cal demanded in a rough tone. "Because if you are, you're a pretty sorry bastard."

"Chill, Cal. I wouldn't jerk your chain about something this serious." Hammond ran his fingers through his thinning gray hair and narrowed his eyes. "Like I just told you, you're a father. *You* have a child. A son, to be exact."

Cal blew out his breath, feeling the color recede from his face followed by an extreme weariness. Since his stint in Colombia, he wasn't anywhere back to his normal self. He tired easily. "Mind if I sit down?"

"Actually, I was about to suggest that." Another smile of sorts crossed the attorney's lips. "I'd hate to think of a grown man hitting my office floor in a dead faint."

Cal gave him a go-to-hell look before practically falling into one of the plush chairs in front of Hammond's massive desk. A million and one questions were charging through Cal's head, but he couldn't seem to process them, much less organize them enough to talk intelligently.

He had a son?

No way.

Couldn't be.

Impossible.

No, not impossible.

A mistake. Pure and simple.

Cal's mood lightened at that last thought, and, forcing himself up straighter in the chair, he hammered his friend with brighter eyes. "It has to be a mistake." A blunt statement of fact.

"You know better than that." Hammond spoke quietly and with conviction.

"But Connie's dead," Cal countered in an argumentative and almost desperate tone. "At least that much leaked through to me."

Hammond gave him one of those exasperated looks. "Your ex was pregnant when she left you but apparently chose to keep that to herself." He paused with a deep sigh. "Happens all the time, which makes the poor chump of a father feel and look like an idiot, when, and if, he ever finds out."

Cal gritted his teeth and at the same time he squeezed

the padded edges of the chair arms until his knuckles turned white. "That bitch," he muttered more to himself than to his friend.

"You knew that when you married her," Hammond pointed out, his brows bunching together, giving him a fierce look.

"You're right, I did." Cal battled his weariness. "Still, I don't know why she chose not to tell me she was pregnant." His tone had regained some of its vibrancy, reeking with pain and anger.

"We both knew she was a piece of work, especially you," Hammond added, again with pointed frankness.

"And I married her anyway." Cal's tone was bleak.

"Well, at least you didn't have to find out about her death and the baby simultaneously." Hammond paused. "If that's any comfort."

Cal's features turned grimmer. "Who was she with when she got killed? I know she wasn't alone."

"After Connie left you, she hooked up with some biker. They were both killed in the accident."

"Were they married?"

"Not that I know of," Hammond responded. "Rumor had them shacking up together."

"Then how do I know the kid's mine?"

"Your name's on the birth certificate," Hammond pointed out bluntly.

Cal lunged out of his chair, reaching for the legal document his attorney held out to him. After perusing the birth certificate, seeing his name stare back at him, he didn't so much as flinch. Instead he walked to the window and stared into the glaring sunshine.

It had been over a year now since he'd been free to do

something as simple as stand in front of a window and not fear for his life. Working undercover as a government investigator forced him to live mostly in the underbelly of society, in the dark and dank places of the drug world.

Before he'd gone undercover, he'd thought of himself as a fairly normal guy—maybe wilder and more headstrong than most. But still normal. Then he'd married Connie Jenkins, and immediately he'd begun to question whether he was normal at all, realizing he'd made the biggest mistake of his life so far.

Now, thank God, he was free to begin his life over, to hope that he had rejoined the ranks of normal people living normal lives. But underneath his outward calm, fear festered. Since he'd been living and dealing with the scum of the earth, he was no longer sure where he belonged or even who he was. Hell, maybe he'd become one of the scumbags himself. Only time would tell.

One thing he did know, he would never go back into the dark, which had nearly driven him over the edge. He winced inwardly, recalling the lighted stick of dynamite that had just been dropped in his lap.

Hell, if this child was his—and he wasn't ready to admit or accept that yet—he wasn't fit to be a parent. He could learn to be, *if* it turned out this baby had his blood flowing through its veins.

He might be a sonofabitch in many ways, but he was never one to shirk his duty, and he wasn't about to start now.

"Cal, are you with me?"

He let go of a pent-up breath, then whipped around and met his friend's inquiring gaze. "My mind's still trying to process what you just told me."

"You can get a DNA test done, of course," Hammond said. "Probably should, since that's within your rights since she lived with another man."

"I could forget you ever told me there was a child." Cal kicked up an eyebrow. "That's also an option. Right?"

Hammond shrugged. "That's your call, of course."

"Only you know I'm not about to do that," Cal said with force. "If my name's on the birth certificate, then he's my child, and I aim to accept the responsibility."

"That doesn't surprise me, my friend. You've never been one to do things by halves. It's all or nothing with you. And that ain't a bad way to be either." Hammond moved his tall, lanky body out of his chair to the bar where he helped himself to a cup of coffee, then gestured to Cal.

Cal shook his head.

After blowing on the liquid, then taking a swig, Hammond added, "On second thought, maybe this is one time you should let sleeping dogs lie, if you get my drift. Maybe you should just walk away from this, start your life over and simply forget about the child. That wouldn't be the worst thing that could happen."

"For me it would," Cal said harshly.

"I'm sorry to hit you with this when you've only been back in town two days. But I wanted you to find out from me rather than the gossip mill. You know how Tyler, Texas, is. It's not quite large enough for people to mind their own business."

"Don't apologize. I had to know, and I'd rather hear it from you than anyone else. At least, I can trust you."

"You can trust a lot of people, Cal." While Hammond's tone was solemn, it also had a confident ring to it. "You have friends who are delighted you're back in civilization."

"I know. It's just going to take me a long time to convince myself of that."

"It's a given you can't discuss what you went through or even where you were, but was it as bad as it appears?"

"Worse than bad," Cal said tersely.

"Well, at least you're done with the whole shebang."

"If this security company gig works out," Cal responded, "I will be for sure."

Hammond sat down and sipped on his coffee. "I thought you'd been hired."

"I have—if I want the job, that is. I have six weeks to make up my mind."

"Even before I told you about the child, I got the impression you were hesitating."

"Hell, Hammond, it's in a foreign country, albeit a safe one."

"So?"

"So, maybe I want to stick around the good ol' U.S. of A. for a while."

"Which tells me you've been out of the country."

Cal narrowed his eyes on his friend. "I didn't say that."

"Okay. Again, I know I'm not privy to anything that pertains to your work, that it's all top-secret mumbo jumbo."

"You're right, so stop fishing."

Hammond's mouth turned up in a half smile. "Just curious, that's all."

"Well, you might as well put a lid on that curiosity because my tenure with Uncle Sam's not something we can ever discuss."

Hammond grinned. "I bet you were damned good at your job, whatever the hell it was. You've always had a reputation for being a real bad-ass."

"You must've been talking to my ex father-in-law." Cal meant that as a sarcastic joke, but when Hammond didn't smile, an alarm bell went off in his head. But then, his brain was trained to pick up on the slightest thing that seemed out of sync.

"Strange that you should say that," Hammond drawled, looking away.

Cal went into full alert mode. "Have you been in contact with Patrick Jenkins?"

"Nope," Hammond said, his gaze returning to Cal.

"I hear a 'but' coming, right?"

"Right." Hammond stared down at his highly polished boots.

"He has the baby," Cal said in a flat, brutal tone.

"Actually it's his daughter, Emma, who has him."

Cal muttered a string of curses.

"I knew you weren't going to like that."

Cal cursed again. "That's an understatement. That bastard hates my guts. And so does his daughter, I'm sure, even though I've never had the pleasure of meeting her." Rich sarcasm accented Cal's every word, for which he made no apologies. He had no use for his ex-wife's family, either. In fact, he'd planned on never having anything to do with them again. Now, though, the dynamics had changed.

"I'm willing to bet you aren't exactly at the top of their friends list either. But then I don't have to tell you that."

Cal rubbed the back of his neck, the muscles so tight they felt like cords of rope—a feeling he had hoped he wouldn't experience again, at least not anytime soon. "Personally I could care less what they think, only—"

"Only now they have something that belongs to you."

"You're damn right."

"I'm glad to hear you say that, Cal." Hammond rose to full height, then ambled over to the coffeepot and refilled his cup. When he looked at Cal again, his usually pleasant features were grim. "For all my earlier posturing, I was afraid that when I told you who had the child, you actually might turn your back and walk away."

"I probably should have."

"No one's twisting your arm. Certainly not me. I'm sure Logan—"

"So that's the kid's name," Cal interrupted, hearing the wonder in his own voice.

"Yep. Maybe it was fate, or what-the-hell ever, but I ran into Jenkins the other day, and he had the boy with him."

"Does he look at all like me?" Cal asked in a halting voice, trying to sort through the myriad of emotions stampeding through him. Damn Connie's hide, he thought, feeling no remorse at all for damning his deceased ex.

If that spoke badly of him, then so be it. He might be a lot of things, but a hypocrite was not one of them. He'd always called a spade a spade, then went for the jugular if the occasion called for it. That was why Uncle Sam had used him to break up one of the government's toughest international drug rings.

But that period in his life was over, Cal reminded himself. Thus, he had to learn to fit into society, even into his ex's family, especially now that they had something that belonged to him. However, the thought of having anything to do with Patrick Jenkins and his daughter made his blood pressure rise and his stomach roil.

"It's hard to tell who a kid looks like, at least for me," Hammond said at last. "Now that you know where Logan is, what's your game plan?"

"Don't have one."

"You can't just appear on their doorstep."

"Why not?"

Hammond rolled his eyes. "That doesn't even deserve an answer."

"The sister's never seen me."

"Which means you're going to start with her?"

Cal shrugged. "Possibly. Right now, I have a lot to digest before I make any move."

"Exactly. And know that I'm here to advise you on the legal side of things."

"Thanks, because I figure it's going to get nasty."

"You can count on that." Hammond set his cup down, then stared directly into Cal's black eyes. "It was obvious that Jenkins thinks the sun rises and sets on that boy. He's not about to give him up without a fight." He paused as if to let those words soak in. "I'm sure the daughter feels the same way."

"What do you know about her, other than her name?" Cal asked.

"She's the owner of a successful plant nursery that supplies the landscaping for her father's works of art."

Cal snorted. "So Patrick's still in the construction business?"

"Yep, and making a fortune, too."

"He was doing that when I was married to Connie. That was part of the problem. She was Daddy's fair-haired princess who had everything handed to her on a silver platter."

"Apparently Emma's not like her at all, but then who knows? I certainly don't. All I have to go by are rumors concerning the rich and affluent, which includes the Jenkinses."

Cal snorted again. "Those people are poison and if I had my way, I'd stay as far away from them as possible."

"I'm sorry you have to step out of one hornets' nest into another one."

Cal shrugged again, then strode toward the door. "You do what you gotta do."

As if he realized the meeting had come to an end, Hammond shot out his hand. "Let me hear from you."

"Oh, you can bet on that."

"Meanwhile, take it easy, get yourself reacquainted with the decent people of the world."

"Yeah, right," Cal muttered, then made his way out the door.

Only when he was behind the wheel of his new pickup did he take a breath. Even at that, it was a harsh one. Then he slammed his palm onto the steering wheel, frustration washing over him.

What the hell was he going to do? He wanted to see his son, yet he didn't. God, the responsibility of just knowing he had a child was overwhelming, especially now. After what he'd been through, he was in no shape to take on a child, not when every time he closed his eyes, he saw a gun aimed at his temple while someone laughingly played Russian roulette with his life.

Suddenly Cal broke out in a cold sweat and felt sick. If he hadn't been driving in a public place, he would've pulled over, opened his door, and emptied the contents of his stomach onto the pavement. But somehow, he found the wherewithal to pull himself together enough so that the nausea passed and his elevated heart rate settled.

Okay, life had dealt him another blow—a personal one, which made it harder for him to deal with—but he was up to the task. If Connie had truly borne him a son, then hell or high water wasn't going to keep him from at least seeing him. Anything else—well, he'd have to cross that bridge when he came to it.

The first thing was to get a plan. No big deal. Planning was what he did best. The Jenkinses didn't know what was about to hit them. He had never backed down from a challenge and he wasn't about to now. For the first time since he'd surfaced back in civilization, he had a purpose in life.

And it felt damn good.

Two

What a lovely early spring day.

Emma paused and peered at a blue Texas sky that didn't have one cloud marring its beauty. She could not have asked for better weather, especially for a person who made her living working outdoors with plants. In all honesty, though, she rarely did any of the manual labor. She owned the nursery and the business side of it kept her tied to the desk.

However, there were days, like this one, when she made the opportunity to wander through her domain and smell the roses—so to speak—and tweak plants, wallowing in self-satisfaction over what she had accomplished.

Of course, her father had had a lot to do with the success of Emma's Nursery. He had given her the capital to get started several years ago—capital that she'd already paid back. But it had been her hard work that had built the business to its present success. Once she made up her mind about anything that was important to her, she wouldn't give up or give in.

"You're stubborn and hard-headed to a fault, girl," her daddy was always telling her, though she knew he admired her tenacity because he was the same way.

"Yeah, girl, you're a chip off the old block."

Thinking of her dad, Patrick, brought a wobbly smile to Emma's lips. While she certainly hadn't been the fair-haired daughter—Connie had held that honor—at least she, Emma, had always had Patrick's respect.

He'd made millions in his construction company and was three years past retirement age, but he wouldn't have any part of retirement. That word wasn't even in his vocabulary. Work and his grandson were what Patrick lived for.

Thinking about Logan strengthened Emma's smile. More than any career, that baby was what she lived for, as well. He was everything to her, made her life complete.

At thirty-five she was still single and saw no reason to change that, especially now that she had legal guardianship of her sister's child. Oh, there had been a few men in her life, even one special man whom she could have probably married if circumstances had been different. They hadn't been, but she had no remorse or regrets.

If she never had anything else but her work and her sister's child, she would be content forever.

Yeah, life was good and she saw nothing in her future to change that.

"Hey, girl, how's your morning going?"

Emma turned and smiled, but not before stripping off her gloves and giving her daddy a big, sunny smile. "Great. How 'bout you?"

"I'm okay."

Patrick didn't sound or look it, which put a tight squeeze on Emma's heart. Ever since Connie had been killed in a motorcycle accident, she'd become fearful of the unexpected. When Patrick Jenkins was anything other than his calm and collected self, then something was amiss.

This morning she sensed something was definitely amiss. For a few seconds, fear rendered her immobile. However, she tried not to let her anxiety show as she stood on her tiptoes and greeted Patrick with a kiss on his leathery-skinned cheek.

Continuing to hold her council, Emma stood back and looked up at him. At sixty-eight, he was a tall, strapping fellow with a spring in his step.

For years he'd worked alongside his men in the hot boiling sun on the construction sites. Hence, his skin bore the mark of the harsh East Texas sun. Wrinkles were grooved deeply in his face and around his eyes; he always seemed to squint as though still trying to block out the sun. His dark mane was thick and without any gray.

Patrick was a good-looking man and had had more than one opportunity to remarry, but he hadn't. When Emma's mother had died of cancer several years back, Patrick hadn't been interested in remarrying, though Emma hoped that might change. Now that Logan had come into their lives, she seriously doubted it.

The baby was Connie's son and that made him even more special. Patrick had adored his baby daughter and was convinced she could do no wrong, even though she went against his wishes and married a man from the wrong side of the tracks whom he had severely disapproved of. Connie's untimely death had affected him more severely than her mother's.

"Got any coffee made?" Patrick asked into the growing silence.

"Sure." Emma pitched her gloves aside and headed toward the small brick building that housed her office and gift shop.

After entering the large, airy room that smelled of fresh-cut flowers, Patrick pulled up short as a broad smile covered his face. "What's he doing here?"

Emma's gaze followed his to the pallet on the floor where her eighteen-month-old nephew lay sleeping, the ear of his worn teddy bear, Mr. Wiggly, tucked in the baby's mouth.

"He was running a little temp this morning and didn't want me to leave him." Emma broke off with a shrug.

"So you and Janet are taking turns seeing about him." Patrick hadn't asked a question, but rather made a statement.

"Right, although I really don't like bringing him to the shop."

"Once in a while doesn't hurt anything." Patrick continued to peer at his grandson, a worshipful look on his face.

"Except give him the idea he can wrap me around his finger and make a habit of it," Emma countered, also giving Logan an indulgent grin.

Patrick snorted. "That's a given."

Emma gave her father a look. "I know I've spoiled him rotten, but you're a fine one to be talking."

"Hey, you don't hear me arguing. It's like the pot calling the kettle black, I know."

Emma flipped him a grin as she got two cups and filled them with coffee. Once they were seated, they sipped in silence and watched the sleeping child.

Finally, over the rim of her cup, Emma stared at her father. "I sense this isn't just a social call."

"It isn't," Patrick admitted with gruff bluntness.

Emma was a bit taken aback, feeling another surge of fear. "What's wrong?"

"Nothing's wrong. At least I hope not."

"Then what's got that look on your face?" Emma pressed.

"Cal Webster."

Emma's hands began to tremble. Before she spilled the contents of the cup, or, better yet, dropped it on the floor, she set the cup down and stared at Patrick through wide, horrified eyes. "What about him?"

"He's back in town."

Patrick said the word *he* as though it were contaminated.

Emma's hand flew to her heart at the same time her gaze bounced back to the baby who remained sound asleep. "Oh, my God," she finally wheezed.

Patrick rose, then sat back down.

It had been a long time since she'd seen her father so agitated—not since the day of Connie's senseless death. He really hadn't been agitated then. *Devastated* was a better word. And furious, too—the same fury she saw twist his features now.

"Dad—" The saliva dried up in her mouth, making further speech impossible.

"I don't think there's cause for panic," Patrick said in that same gruff tone. "Not yet, anyway."

"How can you say that?" Emma's voice rose several decibels.

"I heard the news from a friend who actually saw him about town." Patrick paused and gave Emma a direct stare. "I don't think he knows about Logan."

"You don't think?" Emma stood and began pacing the floor, feeling as if jumping beans were having a field day inside her. "Think is not definitive enough for me."

"I'm working on it, Emma. Just give me time. But from what I know of Cal Webster, if he had the slightest suspicion I had his son, he would've already knocked on my door."

"Oh, Daddy, I don't mean to panic. It's just that when I think of losing—"

Patrick held up his hand, aborting the rest of her sentence, then patted her on the arm. "Don't go there. At least not now. But rest assured, even if he does find out, that bastard won't get to first base. He's already taken one person I love away from me, and I can damn well promise you he's not going to take another one."

Since Patrick had delivered his news, Emma felt her body relax. One rarely crossed her daddy and got by with it. He had clout in this town and wasn't afraid to use it. Sometimes she wondered if he played dirty pool in order to get his way or to make a deal, but since she had no proof, she refused to dwell on the negative.

It was fruitless, anyway. She had enough intuitiveness to realize she couldn't change him or his way of operating. Nor did she want to. In this case, she definitely didn't. She'd make any sacrifice, or do most anything to keep Logan, which she guessed put her in the same class with her father.

"What do we do?" she finally asked, trapping Patrick's dark eyes.

"Nothing."

"Nothing?"

"That's right. It's up to Webster to make the first move.

Why alert him to the fact he has a child? I'm betting a kid is the last thing he'd want to be saddled with. When he was married to your sister, he was wild as a March hare and not afraid of the devil himself."

"That's why I can't believe she married someone like him." Emma shivered. "A kid off the streets."

"A hoodlum is what I called him," Patrick responded grimly. "His dad was a no-good layabout who finally drank himself to death. I think his mother later died from sheer laziness."

"No wonder he was wild," Emma said in a sad tone.

"That's no excuse," Patrick flared back, a muscle in his jaw working overtime.

"Still, that's probably what attracted him to Uncle Sam." Emma shivered again. "No telling what he did for them."

"We'll never know," Patrick said. "But then, I don't give a damn. I just don't want to ever lay eyes on the s.o.b. again."

Emma sighed deeply. "It's a good thing I never had the pleasure of meeting him."

When her sister had hooked up with Cal Webster, Emma had been in Europe studying. By the time she'd returned, the marriage was over and Webster had disappeared.

"The first time your sister brought him home," Patrick was saying, "I knew he was bad news. He was cocky and arrogant even when he didn't have a pot to pee in or a window to throw it out of."

Knowing this conversation had dredged up painful memories, Emma crossed the room and placed a hand on her dad's arm. "It's okay. Like you said, he's probably just passing through, then he'll be gone on another assignment, no telling where."

"That had better be the case," Patrick said with twisted features and venom in his voice.

Before Emma could say anything else, Logan cried out. Turning, she ran to the pallet and dropped to her knees beside him. "Hey, sweetheart," she said with a smile. "Mommy's here. And so is Papa."

"Hey, fellow," Patrick said, making his way to his grandson where he placed a hand on the child's head and tousled his dark hair. "Be a good boy for Mommy today, and I'll take you to get an ice cream cone tonight."

"Ice cream," Logan repeated, a grin on his face.

Facing Emma, Patrick said, "I'll see you two later. I have a meeting in about five minutes."

She nodded. "Keep me posted."

Patrick's features remained twisted. "That goes without saying."

Once he was gone, Emma clutched Logan so tightly to her breast that he began to whimper. "Sorry, son, didn't mean to hurt you." She tweaked him on the chin, then placed a hand on his forehead, which felt cool and free of any fever.

"Mama," he said with his toothy grin.

"Oh," she said wide-eyed. "I hear Mickey's truck."

"Truck," Logan mimicked, his grin increasing.

"That's right, which means Mama has to go. You stay with Janet, and I'll be back in a minute."

As if on cue, her helper came around the corner and took the baby, whose lower lip began to tremble. "Oh, honey, it's okay. Janet will play with you."

Logan kicked his legs, then looped his arms around

Emma's neck and gave her a gooey kiss on the cheek.
Emma laughed with joy as she walked outside.

Cal wasn't sure this was a good idea at all. In fact, it
was probably insanity at its highest level. Still, he'd made
up his mind to go through with this bizarre plan, and he
wasn't about to change it now. Besides, it was too late. He
was already parked in front of his ex sister-in-law's
nursery, his truck loaded with plants.

He was sweating as though he'd been chopping wood,
to his chagrin. Albeit the spring day was hotter than usual,
but he shouldn't have been wet with sweat. Dammit, he
was nervous. He almost laughed out loud at the absurdity
of the situation. He'd been in the worst hellholes one could
imagine, and here he was about to face an innocent woman
and he couldn't function.

Only he knew she wasn't just any woman. She was his
son's guardian.

Dammit, he had to get hold of himself or he couldn't
even get out of the truck, much less rein in his splattered
emotions. Losing control was not something he had
patience with. That could get him dead.

That sudden trek back into the past brought on a curse
as Cal lunged out of the truck, making him aware that
while he might be out of the jungle physically, he had a
long way to go before he was out mentally.

He'd hold that thought and dissect it another time.

Right now, he had other fish to fry. Grabbing his clipboard, Cal made his way around the front of the vehicle.
When he saw Emma coming toward him, he pulled up
short.

While she was not nearly as attractive as Connie had

been, it was obvious they were sisters. Both had the same shaped face and eyes, though their eyes were different colors. And the mouth—there was a resemblance there, too.

But that was where the likeness ended. The closer Emma came, the closer he stared with far more interest than necessary, especially since he had sworn off women.

Most Southern women he knew would never be caught dead without makeup. Emma Jenkins was the exception, and it served her well. Her skin appeared soft and radiant and wrinkle-free, though he knew she was in her mid-thirties. You go girl, he thought; buck the status quo.

But it was the way she was dressed that really captivated his attention. She had on a pair of bright-purple overalls with loose-fitting straps. Underneath was a skimpily-cut T-shirt that hugged her well-endowed breasts and left a smidgen of her ribs bare. He'd bet his last red cent that she was braless. On closer observation, she didn't need one.

Those breasts were upright and perky....

Whoa, cowboy! It had been a long time since he'd noticed a woman's breasts with any interest whatsoever. And he wasn't about to start with her—his ex-wife's sister. God forbid.

Cal dragged his eyes off her chest and back to her face. Unlike Connie, she wasn't beautiful in the true sense of the word, nor was she as blatantly sexy. Yet in her own right, she was lovely. And classy.

She was tall—he'd guess five feet eight—with dark hair worn in a short, bobbed style, which accented her creamy skin and full lips. But it was her eyes that held him

spellbound. They were a unique color—Windex-blue—
and surrounded by an abundance of sooty lashes.

"Mickey, it's about time you got here." She paused, a
frown marring her brows. "You're not Mickey," she
added inanely.

"No, ma'am," Cal drawled, "I'm not."

"Where's Mickey?" she asked bluntly, her eyes giving
him the once-over.

He wondered what she was thinking. If he were to
hazard a guess, he probably wouldn't like it. In no way
would he come near measuring up to her expectations, remembering his reflection in his mirror this morning.

His hair was too long and his jeans and T-shirt both had
holes in them. And his face—well, that was another story
altogether. He knew he looked drawn and disheveled—not
at all pleasing to the eyesight. But give him time, he told
himself. When he had to, he cleaned up real well. He just
hadn't had the time or the inclination to do so.

"I understand he's now on another route. I read about
the vacancy in the paper."

She leaned her head to one side and gave him a suspicious look, like she wanted to say more. She didn't,
though, at least not about Mickey. "So who are you?"

Cal hesitated for a moment, then shot out his hand, a
hearty smile on his lips. "Bart McBride. But my friends
call me Bubba."

Three

Wow!

That was the first thought that came to Emma's mind when she met his eyes, dark and direct. She'd had lots of delivery guys since she'd been in this business, but none had ever looked like this one. She couldn't exactly say he was the best-looking thing that had come down the pike— that would be an exaggeration—yet there was something about him that definitely got her attention.

When it came to men, that wasn't an easy feat.

Maybe it was the hard, dangerous look he seemed to wear so comfortably. Jeez Louise, Emma thought, swallowing nervously, feeling a fluttering of butterflies in her stomach. Who was he? More to the point, how could she have such an irrational reaction to a stranger? A truck driver, to boot.

She wasn't a snob—that wasn't it at all. It usually took

more than a tall, tanned, muscular man with salt-and-pepper hair to make her take a second look.

This time she'd taken more than one look, for heaven's sake. Her eyes were camped on him. Even though she felt color seep into her cheeks, Emma still didn't turn away. Maybe it was those kick-ass dimples in his cheeks that were the culprit. Or maybe it was his even white teeth that appeared even whiter under his tanned skin.

So he was an awesome specimen of manhood. A moment's worth of eye candy. *So what?* She'd been exposed to his type before, and it hadn't come close to striking a nerve.

Why now?

He certainly wasn't her type; that was a given. Much too rough around the edges, too menacing to suit her. In the mounting silence, instead of averting her gaze, however, she perused his body. Her eyes started with his faded and tight-fitting T-shirt, then traveled down to his jeans that had no chance of hiding the impressive bulge of his sex or the powerful strength of his legs.

Emma's flush deepened, and her skin prickled.

Realizing how crazily she was behaving, how totally out of the norm this was, she jerked her eyes back up, but not before she caught the same look of blatant appreciation and interest mirrored in his.

To her dismay, the air around them turned suffocating with sexual tension.

"I'm assuming you're Emma Jenkins," he said, finally.

His low, sandpaper-edged voice now seemed as sexy as his appearance. For another moment, she was speechless, trying to assimilate her feelings. What was this all about? What was *she* all about?

Nothing, she told herself, feeling a surge of defiance flood through her. She was just reacting to a good-looking man, that was all—something she hadn't done in a long time. While that felt good, it also scared the bejesus out of her as her sister's lifestyle flashed before her eyes.

Emma cleared her throat and forced herself to say, "Uh, that's right." He didn't extend his hand again, which was good in light of her crazy reaction to him.

Nope, touching him would definitely not work, mainly because she wanted to. Emma gritted her teeth, then pasted a smile on her face. "I hope everything's okay with Mickey," she commented, trying to lessen the tension that was threatening to mount again. "He was here so often, we actually became friends." She paused. "I'm surprised he didn't tell me he'd been reassigned."

"Oh, I'm sure he'll get around to that," Bubba drawled, peering down at his clipboard, then back up. "Everything in my truck belongs to you."

"That's not a surprise."

"You must have a super business."

"I do."

Bubba grinned, which played more havoc with her insides. "Can't beat that. So I guess we'll be seeing a lot of each other."

Oh, brother. "Not if Mickey comes back."

"I don't think there's much chance of that, at least not for a while."

"If you see him, tell him to stop by and see me, okay?"

"Sure will."

A silence.

This time Bubba cleared his throat and was apparently about to say something when Emma heard a noise behind her. She swung around and saw Logan, pursued by a ha-rassed-looking Janet, come toddling toward her.

"I'm sorry, Em, but he got away from me."

Emma smiled, reached for Logan and swept him into her arms. After flicking him on the chin, she said with a grin, "You're a bad boy."

"Bad," Logan mimicked, hugging her around the neck as he took a peek at Bubba.

"Good-looking kid."

"Thanks."

"He's yours, right?" Bubba asked.

Not wanting to get personal with this man made Emma hesitate, then she thought of Mickey. When he'd asked that same question, she hadn't been reluctant to respond at all. Just the opposite, in fact. With this Bubba character, it was another matter altogether.

Her reaction wasn't because he'd asked about Logan *per se,* but because *she* had reacted to Bubba so strongly and wanted him to take care of business and be on his way.

Yet she wanted him to stay. How much sense did that make? None. Again, she had never reacted to a man in such a forthright way. Bluntly put, she was intrigued, much to her dismay.

Then realizing how absurd, how out-of-hand her thoughts had gotten, Emma declared in a firm, but busi-nesslike tone, "Yes, he is." Then she hesitated and with a proud smile added, "Or at least he soon will be."

"Care to explain?" he asked.

Slightly taken aback by his continued boldness, Emma plastered another smile on her face and said, "Not at the moment."

Bubba laughed, then winked. "Before I wear out my welcome, I guess I'd best unload this truck and move on."

"I think that's a grand idea."

Bubba paused and looked her up and down again, leaving her breathless in her tracks. He then walked to the back of the truck, shoved up the big door and went about his task.

When he finished, he brought the invoice for her to sign, placing her in much closer proximity to him than she would have liked. Despite the warmth of the morning, the smell of soap still clung to his skin; it wafted through her senses, creating another cluster of butterflies in her tummy.

If this man didn't hurry up and get out of her sight…

"Be seeing you, Emma," Bubba said with a grin that recalled her attention to those kick-ass dimples.

"I'm sure you will." She watched him climb into the truck. "Thanks."

He nodded. "You bet." Then added, "Take care of that boy, you hear?"

Until he disappeared, she stood her ground, feeling as if her bones had turned to water, leaving her weak and unsteady. And damned confused. Finally she hauled a heavy Logan back inside, but even that seemed like an effort.

Once the baby was back under the tutelage of Janet, Emma went into her office, closed the door, sat down in her chair and took several deep breaths, trying to quiet her erratic heartbeat.

"Stop it," she muttered aloud, grabbing the invoice and pen, forcing herself to peruse the statement. If the truth be known, while her fingers were doing their job, her mind was not. It was elsewhere, she conceded, a mutinous curve to her mouth. It was on that driver. There was something about him that had an effect on her.

Stop it, she repeated silently, having sworn long ago not to become a clone of her sister. She almost laughed at the thought, it was so ludicrous. Even if she'd wanted to, it wouldn't have been possible.

Connie was like a true princess, tiny and blond with a figure to die for. Enhancing that lovely body was a bubbly personality. She attracted people, especially men, like bees to honey. But underneath that Southern belle demeanor was a wild streak that Connie had never learned to control.

Men seemed to have loved that in her. Not only were they attracted to her, but she to them. Not so with Emma. The fact that she didn't have the same appetite for the opposite sex always brought ridicule from her sister.

Connie had continually pointed out, "God, you're such a stick-in-the-mud, sis."

"I'm sorry you feel that way," Emma had responded in as calm a tone as possible.

"No, you're not. That's what makes it so bad." Connie smiled her sunny smile and batted her big dark lashes. "Why don't you let me fix you up? We'll double-date, and I'll show you how to have the time of your life."

"Thanks, but I'll pass," Emma said with a smidgen of defiance, which Connie readily picked up on.

"What's your problem?" Connie demanded in an ugly tone. "You gay, or something?"

That barb cut to the core. Still, Emma kept her cool, knowing that Connie thrived on a good verbal fight, determined to win no matter what. Having learned that early on, Emma merely smiled and said, "You know better than that, Connie. I just prefer to pick my own men, that's all."

Connie gave an unladylike snort, then mouthed off, "Yeah, right."

A deep heavy sigh parted Emma's lips, bringing her out of her morbid thoughts back into the sunlight. Connie was gone and it was pointless to let herself dwell on the bad times, though she had to confess there were few good ones.

While she knew that Patrick loved her, he had adored Connie. He'd tried not to show his partiality, but he hadn't pulled it off. Patrick's adoration remained on course even after Connie had married, divorced and even got hooked on drugs. Once the baby was born, she couldn't stand being tied down. Not long after that, she took up with a biker. It was then that she had made Emma her baby's guardian. They never saw Connie again except in her casket.

That child had been the only thing that had kept Patrick from falling apart after Connie's death. Realizing that her mind had once again backtracked into the morbid, Emma lunged up and took several calming breaths.

She had made peace with Connie's death. Out of that peace had come the certainty that she would never end up like her sister, who couldn't control her lust for a man.

A wail almost erupted from Emma's lips. Hadn't she done the very same thing this morning? Lust had shot through her when she'd first seen Bubba McBride. Why? Because he'd made her feel like a woman for the first time in her life. How crazy was that? Most likely he was married with a home in suburbia with two-point-three children, even though he hadn't been wearing a wedding ring. However, a ringless finger didn't mean anything.

Gritting her teeth again, Emma shoved the thought of that stranger out of her mind and went in search of Logan. When things in her life began to get out of kilter, the responsibility of him put her back on solid ground.

Thank God.

* * *

He'd never lacked balls before. Why this morning? Why hadn't he told Emma Jenkins who he was?

Cal had asked himself that question countless times and still hadn't come up with an answer worth a damn. *Bubba?* His mouth twisted. God, where had that idiotic name come from? He had no idea; it had crossed his mind and he'd blurted it out. Now his foot was stuck in his mouth and it sure didn't taste good.

What now?

That was the really big question, the one he had no choice but to answer. Only not right now. He was too busy controlling the sick feeling churning in the pit of his stomach. Finally, he reached the gates of his ranch several miles north of Tyler.

His mother and dad had left him this prime piece of property only because they hadn't gotten around to selling it before their deaths. Cal's lips twisted sardonically, remembering his parents and how unimportant he'd been to them.

If he hadn't run away from home and joined the army, he'd probably be dead by now. He would've joined a gang and been sucked into the same underworld he'd spent much of his adult life fighting.

Thank God that hadn't happened and thank God he had this place.

It was home to him now, especially since he loved the outdoors, reveling in the freedom it gave him. Until his new security job took him out of the country, he aimed to spend as much time here with his horses and cattle as he could.

He just wished he could bring his son....

Cal slammed on the brakes and shoved the gearshift in

Park, feeling sweat ooze out of every pore in his body. He was also dizzy. He rested his head on the steering wheel until it stopped spinning.

His child.

His son.

By damn, he was a father.

Of a fine-looking boy, too. When he'd first laid eyes on the kid, he'd been awestruck, thinking Logan couldn't be his flesh and blood. No way could he and Connie, out of the misery of their marriage, have produced a tiny being so perfect. Hence, the kid had to have come from someone else's loins.

Then just as quickly Cal's negative thoughts turned a bit positive when he remembered a baby picture of himself he'd found at the ranch. Logan did resemble the kid in the picture.

Screw DNA testing; he didn't need that. Logan was his kid.

Still shaking, Cal swiped the sweat from his brow and above his lip. He remained too shaken to drive toward the small cabin that served as his home. His gaze searched for his foreman, Art Rutherford, who was usually out and about taking care of chores. When Cal didn't see Art or his vehicle, relief flooded through him.

Right now he didn't want to see or talk to anyone. He had some serious thinking to do. Since he'd lied to Emma Jenkins, he might as well see where that took him. Maybe if he wormed his way into her good graces, she would let him see the kid. In doing that, he had to know he might run head-on into her father, who would immediately recognize him, and the gig would be up.

If that happened, he'd devise plan B. That was his boy and no one was going to take Logan away from him.

"Whoa, brother," he said out loud, "Don't go gettin' too big for your britches."

While getting his son, having something of his own for the first time in his life, might be his top priority, he had to ask himself a brutal and honest question. How equipped was he to become a parent? He had a ton of emotional baggage weighing him down, which certainly didn't make him parent material.

The Jenkinses knew that and were sure to use it against him. Both father and sister hated him with a passion. To add insult to injury, Connie's sister had built a smoldering fire in his loins.

Not a good thing.

Though a chill of foreboding shot through him, Cal couldn't ignore this emotional upheaval. Like it or not, seeing Emma today had made him think thoughts he hadn't had since he'd returned from Central America. But Emma was different. She fascinated him because she had no idea how attractive, how sexy, she was.

He'd never met a female who seemed as unaware of herself as she was. There was nothing artificial about her, no desire to be noticed. She reeked of sexuality, with a fragile innocence that any man in his right mind would have found appealing.

Any man but him, he told himself savagely. He wasn't about to get involved with any woman, especially not his ex-sister-in-law, who had every intention of taking his child away from him.

So what was he doing counting the days until he could return to the nursery?

Four

"Ms. Jenkins, this is a disaster. Plain and simple."

And you're a bitch. Now where had that ugly thought come from? Emma asked herself, appalled at the direction her mind had taken. Granted, Sally Sue Landrum was a pain in the rear, but she hadn't earned the title of bitch. Not yet, anyway.

"No, it's not a disaster, Sally," Emma rebutted with all the patience she could muster. "I told you I'd have your landscaping finished today, and I intend to keep that promise."

Sally pursed her full lips, placed her hands on her tiny waist and glared at Emma. "That won't happen without plants."

"I'll get the plants." Emma's tone held conviction, even though she wasn't sure she could follow through, which would indeed be a disaster.

She didn't take many private jobs because her daddy

kept her so busy with his projects. But there had been a lull in her business right now, so when her friend Sally had called and practically begged her to landscape the grounds of her new multi-million dollar home, Emma had said yes.

Actually, she'd been thrilled, seeing a home as something different, and as a challenge. At the moment, with Sally glaring at her, she was beginning to rue the day she'd taken the job.

Dammit, the supplier had told her just yesterday the plants she'd ordered would be in. So far, that hadn't come to fruition. She'd called other suppliers, but none could fill her need. To make matters worse, Sally was having a big open house to show off her new mansion, which put that much more pressure on Emma.

"Sally, go back inside and do whatever it is you do," Emma said into the hostile silence, "and let me handle things on this end." She paused and forced a smile. "Please."

Sally was having no part of Emma's smile; that was apparent by the tightening of her lips. "You're my friend, Emma. You of all people, I thought I could count on."

"You can." Emma's tone was terse. "Again, just leave me alone and let me do my job. Everything will be all right."

"It had better be."

With that, Sally flounced around and marched back into the mansion, slamming the door behind her. Emma breathed for the first time since she'd been accosted by her friend and client, then reached for her cell phone and dialed her main supplier.

"Fred, this is—"

"I know who it is."

"Have my plants come in yet?"

"Yes, praise the Lord."

Emma wilted on the spot, the relief washing through her was so acute.

"Thank you, Fred."

"Don't thank me."

"Why not?"

"Thank Bubba McBride. He's the one responsible."

"Oh?" she said inanely, her heart pounding slightly harder, which was crazy. Even the man's name had an effect on her. This foolishness had to come to an end.

"He volunteered to go after them, and I told him to hit the road."

Following another deep, settling breath, Emma said, "When do you expect him back?"

"He's on his way to the estate, even as we speak."

"I owe you, Fred. And Bubba," she emphasized before snapping her cell shut.

It was then that she heard the squeal of brakes. Whipping around, she watched Bubba bound out of the truck and saunter toward her. She tried not to react to his dark, menacing good looks, but nothing short of another miracle would've stopped that.

At the moment, she was fresh out of miracles.

"Hiya," he said in that low, sexy voice that scraped across her skin like fingernails over a chalkboard. Emma shivered. And that look in his eyes—she couldn't ignore that either.

For a moment, she stiffened under that gaze, more potent than the sun bearing down on her head. Then her sanity came to her rescue. No matter how captivating he might be—and she couldn't deny that he was—she wasn't interested.

Then why was she fixated on the width of his muscled shoulders and the span of his six-pack abs? She dared not look any farther south, already knowing the power he packed there.

"Hi yourself," she responded but not before swallowing hard, feeling suddenly like a teenager meeting a new beau. God, how corny—and ridiculous. She was a grown woman with a child. Where were her good sense and her pride?

Pulling herself together, Emma wiped the answering smile off her face and said in her most businesslike tone, "I spoke to Fred and he told me what you did. Thanks a lot."

A mocking smile answered her formality, which merely added to that sexiness he wore like a second skin. And those dimples, they were definitely bad on a woman who was trying to keep her heart out of the equation.

"You're welcome," he said, that mocking smile still intact.

"Okay, so you saved my rear," she added with more punch.

"Glad I could oblige. Now, shall we get down to work?"

Emma gave him a startled look. "I have a crew, Bubba. Besides, I'm sure you have other deliveries to make."

"Not this afternoon. So put me to work, and we'll get this job done."

Though Emma was tempted to argue, she refrained. One thing, another pair of hands would help, and she wanted his company. Hold it, girl, she warned. She was headed for deep waters and if she was not careful, she'd drown. Still...

"Tell me what you want me to do," Bubba said, jerking

her mind back to the moment at hand. "And we'll have this job done before you can spell Rumpelstiltskin."

She laughed then. "That's where you're wrong. I have a child, remember?"

"Ah, right, you do," he responded, his tone becoming serious. Then, before anything else could be said, he turned and went about the task of unloading the plants.

A little past mid-afternoon, the biggest part of the grounds were planted. Emma couldn't remember the last time she'd been this exhausted. Usually, she only supervised, letting her crew do the manual labor. But since Bubba was working like a field hand, she pitched in and did her share of digging and planting.

Surprisingly, she'd enjoyed every minute of it. She'd forgotten how much fun it was to dig in the dirt.

"So, what do you think?" Bubba asked, sidling up to her while wiping the sweat off his face with a handkerchief from the back pocket of his cutoffs. Although he smelled sweaty, he wasn't offensive. In fact, she ached to reach for the rag and blot the sweat off herself. Emma cringed at her thoughts.

The effect this man had on her was uncanny and just plain unnerving.

"Well?" he pressed when she didn't answer.

"It looks awesome, and I can't thank you enough."

"Sure you can."

"How?" she asked before she thought.

"Let me fix you a glass of the best lemonade you've ever drunk." He paused. "At my place."

"Look, I can't, really. I have to pick up Logan from the daycare."

"He can come, too. Children like lemonade."

She gave him a look. "I don't—"

"Please," he said in a cajoling tone. "It's been a long, hot day. We both need a treat." He paused and gave her another one of those heart-stopping smiles. "What can it hurt?"

Nothing, except to get me all rattled inside for no good end, Emma thought.

"All right, I'm game," she finally said, ignoring her conscience and knowing, too, she would probably regret this outing.

What the heck? She hadn't been attracted to a man in a long time and while she knew nothing would ever come of the two of them, it might be fun to test the waters. Just because she suddenly wanted to enjoy a male's company didn't make her into a man-lover like her sister. She just needed to chill.

Thirty minutes later, after they had swapped trucks and picked up Logan, they were headed toward the outskirts of town. "So where are we going?" she asked, feeling a bit uneasy.

"To my place."

Her stomach somersaulted. "And where is that?"

"It's not much farther."

At least Logan was quiet, sleeping in her arms after long hours at the daycare—one that believed in working their little bodies as well as their little minds. Logan attended three days a week, which she thought was ample. She didn't want to be away from him more than that.

"He seems to be such a good kid."

"He is." Emma smiled. "The best."

"Here we are," Bubba said, before turning onto a blacktop road that eventually led to a small cabin surrounded by some of the biggest and most beautiful oak trees she'd ever seen. Her breath caught at the splendor before her.

"Hey, this is awesome," she exclaimed, facing his profile. That was when she saw a bead of sweat dribble down the exposed cheek. She literally fought the urge to lick it off.

Horrified yet again at her wanton thoughts, Emma jerked her eyes off him, but not before she felt her face turn crimson. Thank God he couldn't read her mind, or she'd be in deeper trouble than she already was.

Reality. She should not have come.

"Hey, it's okay. I'm harmless."

She jerked back around and knew her face was still crimson. No way could he not see that. "I would hope so," she snapped.

The corners of his lips merely twitched, then he said, "Come on, let's go in."

Once inside, he headed straight for what she figured was the guest bedroom. She followed. There he reached for the still-sleeping baby and placed him in the middle of the bed. While she looked on in speechless wonder, he placed pillows on either side of the child.

"There," he said, turning to Emma. "How'd I do?"

"Great," she responded, feeling rather helpless. This man was something else.

Moments later they were in the bright and airy kitchen. "Have a seat at the bar," he said, "while I whip up the lemonade."

Still feeling like a fish out of water, something foreign to her, Emma did as she was told.

Soon they were sipping the sweet/tart liquid out of frosty mugs, listening to the birds outside sing. For a moment, Emma felt as though she was in another world. The country was something she didn't have much use for, always having been a curb-and-gutter girl. But gosh, she couldn't deny how nice it was here, especially when she looked out over a huge pond spotted with white ducks.

Logan would love watching them. Thinking of the child, she slipped off the bar stool and said, "I'll be right back. I'm going to check on my baby."

"I assume he's still sleeping," Bubba said when she took her place beside him seconds later.

She nodded with a smile. "Out like a light, in fact. They wore his little tush out at daycare."

"So how often do you put him there? Every day?"

"Oh, no. I wouldn't dream of that. I have full-time help at the nursery, which makes it possible for me to stay home with him some days."

"So the daycare's kind of optional?"

"You might say that."

He smiled before taking another sip of his lemonade.

She cut him a glance, more curious than ever about a man who drove a plant truck but owned a spread like this. The two simply didn't jive.

"What about you?" She noticed him stiffen, upping her curiosity.

"What about me?"

Emma shrugged. "For starters, are you married?" She couldn't believe she'd asked that, especially since it wasn't any of her business.

"No. But that should be a given since you're here with me."

"You never know," she said more to herself than to him.

"I could ask you that same question."

"You know I'm not married," she said with an unexpected sharpness.

"No, not really."

"Well, I'm not," she declared.

A silence followed during which she felt his eyes appraise her as though trying to figure out what was going on inside her head. In doing that, he didn't bother to hide the fire that sprang into his eyes.

Out of self-defense, Emma avoided further eye contact, then asked, "Have you ever been married?" she pressed, mostly because he seemed so reluctant to answer that question.

His lips tightened, forming a straight line. "Once."

"I see."

"I doubt that, but it's okay. It's something I don't like to talk about."

"Most men don't." Emma couldn't quite keep the sarcasm out of her voice.

His eyebrows kicked up. "Ouch."

She grinned. "Sorry, that was uncalled for."

Another silence, then he asked, "How do you like your lemonade?"

"It's the best."

"Good."

Emma cast him another glance. "You haven't always driven a plant truck, have you?"

He sighed. "You don't give up, do you?"

"I don't know what you're talking about," she said with faked innocence.

"Sure," he muttered with a down-turned mouth.

"Okay, so I'm curious."

"You're right. I haven't always driven a truck. Actually, I do security work."

"Mmm, that's interesting."

"You're right, it is, so let's leave it at that for now, okay?"

Emma shrugged again. "Suit yourself. It doesn't matter, anyway," she said in an offhanded manner, letting him know that she didn't really give a damn what he did. The sooner he figured that out the better for both of them.

"Hey," he said softly, "look at me."

"I don't think that's a good idea," she answered in a muffled voice.

An awkward and tense silence filled the room.

"I think it's time I went home." She toyed with a strand of her hair. "It's getting late, plus it's time to feed Logan."

He got up and faced her directly. "Thanks for coming. I enjoyed the hell out of your company."

Emma was taken aback, certain she'd hacked him off with her probing questions. Apparently not, which made him more intriguing than ever.

He winked at her. "Come on, let's get the kid."

She followed, all the while wondering what the hell kind of emotional soup she'd jumped into with this man.

Five

He was one grateful man.

Emma's Nursery was one thriving business, which worked right into his plans. Not that he had a plan, he reminded himself with a twinge of guilt.

Getting a job driving this truck had been an afterthought. Because he'd been desperate to be around his child without raising a red flag and declaring war, he'd thought of every conceivable way to make that happen.

Then a solution had hit him—try a wholesale nursery, only not just any wholesaler, one who called on Emma. Usually, almost all of them needed drivers. Maybe he'd get lucky, which indeed he had.

However, deciding not to tell her who he really was hadn't been planned. Again, it had merely been a knee-jerk reaction. Still, it had worked to his benefit, so far, anyway.

He'd already made a delivery to her shop this morning,

only to wish he had an excuse to return. But his delivery schedule was almost finished for the day, and he was doomed to head back to the warehouse where he didn't want to go.

This morning Cal pulled off the road, his mind buzzing, mostly about seeing her first thing. Emma had been outside watering some plants. He'd pulled up just in time to see her lean over and pluck off several dead leaves. His mouth had watered at the sight of full breasts thrusting against the tight T-shirt.

But it was the provocative swell of her bottom against the cuffed jeans, accentuating the lushness of her hips and thighs, that made him turn as hard as a nightstick.

He'd felt an almost overwhelming urge to jump out of the truck, sneak up behind her and rub his hands over every nook and cranny of that rear. She had looked up then, which had instantly destroyed those insane visions and thoughts.

Suddenly Cal gave his head a violent shake to clear it, reminding himself that his child was what this was all about. Not his libido, and not her, for God's sake.

"You're early," she'd said, standing up straight as he approached her.

"I decided to make you the first stop," he said without further explanation.

"Thanks. I appreciate that." She paused and cocked her head to one side. "I think."

He smiled, then asked, "So how are things?"

"Great," she said, her voice a trifle guarded.

"How's the boy?" He tried to keep his tone light so as not to set off an alarm. Surely that wouldn't be the case, he assured himself. After all, she didn't have a clue who he was or what he wanted. He just had to make sure that held true until *he* was ready to let the cat of the bag, so to speak.

"He's great, too," she said.

"Good."

An awkward silence ensued while they both looked at each other as if they didn't know what to say or do next. He sure as hell didn't. He was wading in water way over his head and knew it. Still, he was willing to tread that water for as long as it took.

Bottom line: he wanted to see his child again. This woman was the key to that happening. If he had to suck up, use all the charm he could muster, then so be it. He'd do whatever it took. He felt badly about deceiving her. Unlike her sister, she was a nice lady, and she deserved better. Unfortunately, though, he didn't have the time or the patience to try and win her over the right way.

When it came to his son, time was not on his side. It was his enemy.

"Uh, let me get Hector to help you unload," she said hastily as if she realized they had been staring at each other for what seemed an interminable length of time. Actually, it had only been seconds.

However, seconds were all Cal needed to feel the burn in his loins from simply looking at her. He couldn't imagine how it would be to touch her. He'd ignite….

"Drop it," Cal muttered under his breath.

"Did you say something?"

"No," he lied.

Her eyes narrowed in disbelief, but she didn't say anything else.

"I guess I'd better take care of business," he said gruffly, turning his back on her.

Once the truck was unloaded and she'd signed the ticket, another silence fell between them. "We're acting like strangers," he said, seeking her gaze and trapping it.

Emma raised her eyebrows as a flush crept over her face. He wasn't sure whether that flush resulted from what he'd said or from the sun beaming down on her face. Either way, it was quite flattering, calling attention to a dusting of freckles across her nose. Funny, he hadn't noticed those yesterday.

"That's because we are," she said in a slightly unsteady tone.

"We could change that. If you want to, that is."

She ran the tip of her pink tongue across her bottom lip. Talk about making him squirm. If she had looked down, she would've seen the effects of that gesture. His erection was threatening to bust through his zipper.

"I'm not sure I want to," Emma said with a soft boldness, still holding his gaze.

"I'll have to see what I can do about that," he drawled, removing his hat and swiping his brow.

"You'll be wasting your time."

Though her answer disappointed him as well as surprised him, it made him realize she was no pushover. But then he shouldn't have been surprised. She wasn't anything like Connie who *had* been a pushover. But then Connie had loved men, all men, and this woman didn't seem to care if she had one in her life or not. While a part of him said kudos to her, another part panicked.

Somewhere deep within, he'd convinced himself that if he got to know her and a trust developed between them, then the truth about him, when it came out, wouldn't be such a shock or a deal breaker.

However, if she wouldn't let him get past that barrier she'd erected, then he was screwed, blued and tattooed. Because of Logan, he couldn't let that happen.

"Thanks," she said, breaking into his thoughts, "for thinking of me first."

"No problem." He paused. "I'll make it the same time in the morning."

She did that little thing with her tongue again. He groaned inwardly.

"I'm not scheduled for anything tomorrow," Emma added.

He winked. "I'll see you anyway."

Emma opened her mouth to respond, but before she could, he jumped back in the truck and drove off. When he looked in the rearview mirror, she was staring at the truck with a pained expression on her face. Better pained than no expression at all, he told himself, another pang of guilt kicking his innards.

Now, still parked on the side of the road, Cal wondered what she'd say if he simply dropped by unannounced with no plants. He scoffed. She'd most likely tell him to take a hike. Then again, maybe not. She wasn't as indifferent to him as she'd like him to believe. And he sure as hell wasn't indifferent to her.

"Give it a rest, Webster," he muttered, jerking the gear-shift into Drive.

A short time later, he turned in his invoices and got into his own vehicle. But instead of heading home, he stopped by Hammond's office, hoping to see him.

Cal was in luck. Hammond had just returned from court and had no other clients scheduled for the day.

"Hey, friend, what's up?" he asked after greeting Cal.

Cal sat down. "Just got off my route."

Hammond's lanky body shook with laughter. "Now that's a hoot. You delivering plants."

"Don't laugh," Cal rebuked with seriousness. "It lets me get acquainted with my ex sister-in-law and my son."

"You're pullin' my leg?"

"Nope."

"So it's *your son* now?"

"That's what I said."

"The other day you were considering a DNA test to prove that."

"I decided that wasn't necessary."

Hammond raised his eyebrows. "Oh?"

"Circumstances have changed."

"And how's that?"

"I told you. My delivery job."

Hammond merely shook his head. "Unbelievable."

"I have to move fast," Cal stressed. "You know I don't have time to let any grass grow under my feet."

Hammond ran a hand over his bald spot. "True, but I still can't believe you've managed to pull that off."

"Well, I did. And is he ever a little pistol," Cal said, unable to contain the excitement in his voice. "But then you know that. You've seen him."

"Most eighteen-month-old kids are," Hammond responded.

"He's damn good-looking, too."

Hammond rolled his eyes. "Aren't you getting a little carried away?"

"He's a chip off the old block, if I ever saw one," Cal continued in that same proud voice.

"So a DNA test is out?"

Cal didn't hesitate. "Yep."

"Like I told you the other day, it's your call." Hammond paused. "What did Emma say when you told her who you were?"

Cal averted his gaze at the same time as he squirmed in his seat. Finally, he looked at his friend and admitted, "I didn't."

Hammond's jaw dropped. Literally. Then he clamped it shut and stared at Cal as though he'd lost his marbles.

"Don't look at me like that," Cal muttered harshly, "like I don't have a brain between my ears."

"As far as I'm concerned you don't, at least not when it comes to that asinine stunt."

Cal gave him a hostile look. "I know what I'm doing, Hammond."

"Really?"

A flush of anger fought with Cal's tan. The flush won the battle. "I told her my name was Bart McBride, but that my friends called me Bubba."

"Bubba?" Hammond laughed without humor. "God, I think I'm going to puke."

Cal lunged out of the chair. "I didn't come here for a lecture, dammit."

"Well, I sure hope you didn't come for absolution, because it's going to take a priest to give you that."

"Funny."

"Wasn't meant to be."

Cal blew out a harsh breath, then forced himself to calm down. He knew Hammond was right. He never should have lied to Emma, but he had and now he had to live with it, at least for a while.

"Look, all I want from you," Cal said, "is advice about my next move."

"Tell the truth."

"Other than that."

Hammond rolled his eyes again. "Do you want your son?"

"Absolutely."

"Full custody?"

"Absolutely."

He blew out a long breath. "That's not going to be easy."

Cal was astonished and didn't bother to hide it. "And just why not? After all, he is my flesh and blood. Why shouldn't the courts give him to me?"

"Before I go into that, I have to ask you something."

"Shoot."

"What kind of parent would you make? Have you asked yourself that?"

A mutinous expression crossed Cal's face. "I could handle it. I'm sure about that."

Hammond snorted.

"You don't think I could?"

"I don't have an opinion one way or the other. I just think it's something you should think about long and hard. It's not easy to take a child and make him into a good citizen. It takes time, energy, patience and a whole lot of love."

"How will I know whether I can be a father until I try?" Cal asked, squashing a feeling of uneasiness.

"I don't suggest you go into this thinking it's a trial run."

"That's not what I meant at all," Cal snapped.

Hammond held up his hands and stepped back. "Hey, I'm not making a judgment one way or the other." He paused. "But the judge will, my friend."

"You know how to go for the jugular," Cal muttered darkly.

Hammond shrugged. "You asked."

"What else?"

"They just don't rip a child out of a mother's arms," Hammond added, "and give him to a virtual stranger who plans to whisk him out of the country into the care of a nanny."

"Emma's not his mother," Cal pointed out defiantly.

"For all practical purposes she is. And she's his legal guardian."

Cal rubbed the back of his neck in frustration. "So I'm between a rock and hard place. I've been there before and gotten out."

"Want me to draw up the legal documents?"

Yes was on the tip of Cal's tongue, only to be swallowed. "Not yet. Let's give my plan a chance to work. It's possible I can gain Emma's trust."

"She's only half the battle. Don't forget about Patrick."

"I haven't. Trust me. But I have to start somewhere. And Emma's the weak link in that chain."

"I hope the hell you know what you're doing, boy."

Cal said in a glum voice, "I hope the hell I do, too."

Again, he had every intention of driving to the ranch. But when he left Hammond's office, he found his vehicle headed in the direction of Emma's Nursery. Since it wasn't quite closing time, he felt sure he would catch her.

Or at least he hoped that was the case. He had no idea what he'd say to explain why he was showing up a second time that day, but he'd cross that bridge when he came to it. He wanted to see his son and he hoped Logan would be with her.

The only problem was, he might tip his hand as to why he was there. He had to be careful not to inquire about the kid too much or Emma might get suspicious. But it was going to be hard to keep his mouth shut.

Damn, what a mess he'd gotten himself into. No. What a mess Connie had gotten him into. If only she'd told him she'd been pregnant, maybe things would've been different. His conscience squealed. He wasn't being entirely fair. Maybe she hadn't known. Even if she had, nothing would've changed, at least not when it came to his assignment. He'd made a commitment to Uncle Sam, and nothing short of his death would have changed that.

Cal muttered a string of curses. If he didn't stop thinking like this, he was going to end up in a rubber room. He'd come close already, and he wasn't about to tip the scales in that direction again.

When he whipped the truck into the parking lot of the nursery, it looked deserted. His feathers withered. Still, he got out and knocked on the door. A few minutes later, Emma responded, a shocked look on her face.

"What are you doing here?"

"I came to see you."

"Why?"

"Are you alone?"

"No." A frown marred her brows. "I have Logan."

"Great."

She gave him an exasperated look. "Why do you say that?"

He paused for a moment, then said in a nonchalant tone, "It's a great day for ice cream in the park. What do you say?"

Six

Emma couldn't believe she'd been so gullible. Again. But she had. The fact that she was sitting in the park with Bubba and Logan bore testimony to that. Sad part about it, she was loving every minute of it.

Especially looking at Bubba. Her eyes soaked him up like a sponge, taking in his cream-colored T-shirt and brown cargo shorts that clung to his muscular legs, emphasizing every bulge they covered. For a mad moment, she envisioned him without those shorts, protruding sex and all, spiking her pulse.

She sucked in her breath and held it. She had to stop thinking like that.

"Man, what a great day," Bubba said, breaking her train of thought.

Indeed it was. The smell of flowers in all varieties, shapes and sizes titillated her senses. High above them in the trees were squirrels playing tag and birds singing their melodious tunes.

Yet it was Logan who seemed to be getting the most pleasure out of the park. He watched the older kids play on the merry-go-round, while laughing and toddling around. He had just finished a cup of ice cream, which he'd smeared from one side of his face to the other.

Bubba could take the credit for that, much to her shock and fascination.

"Do you mind if I feed him?" he'd asked, after they had found a deserted picnic table.

Though there were several parks in the city, this one was Emma's favorite, probably because it was more secluded and didn't have a swimming pool, which made it safer and less congested. She often brought Logan here to read and sing to him.

"Are you sure you don't mind?" Cal asked, narrowing his eyes on her, drawing her attention back to him.

She shrugged. "It's okay with me."

"Guess we'll see what the little fellow thinks about it."

"Pooh," Emma said, flapping her hand. "When it comes to food, especially ice cream, he's a pushover."

"Works for me." Cal grinned at the same time he reached for the small cup of vanilla ice cream that Emma had placed on the table.

"Oops, wait a sec," she said. "I forgot his bib."

"Does he have to have one?"

She laughed. "Are you kidding? Even with it, he'll be a mess." She paused and angled her head. "And you, too."

Cal shrugged. "Won't bother me."

"Don't say I didn't warn you."

He merely grinned, then turned to Logan, and said, "Okay, fellow, it's just you and me and this cup of cream."

Emma had watched in an awed silence as Bubba fed the child. Though it was obvious he'd never had that pleasure, he'd mastered it quickly, never seeming to lose patience when liquid drooled out of both sides of Logan's mouth, or when the baby grabbed the spoon just after Bubba had refilled it.

The way he'd handled the child made her think he'd be a good father. Of course, it wasn't too late. His biological clock had a long time to tick. Meanwhile he could marry and have several children. Probably would, she told herself. For some reason that thought had jabbed at her heart a bit. Then, shaking herself, she'd forced herself to concentrate on the two of them, laughing when Logan rubbed ice cream on Bubba's face.

All three laughed.

Suddenly she felt Bubba's gaze on her, giving her a decidedly sensual appraisal. But it was when his eyes narrowed and dropped to her mouth that a flame ignited in the depths of her stomach.

Logan squealed about that time and broke the spell that held them.

That episode had happened about thirty minutes ago and Emma had made it a point not to let Bubba trap her gaze again. It was far too risky to her peace of mind. But then coming here with this sexy stranger had been risky to begin with. When he'd suggested this trek, she should've said no and meant it.

But when it came to him and her attraction to him, she'd been weak. Even though she condemned herself for that weakness, she couldn't vow she wouldn't succumb again. And she'd make no apologies for it, either.

Suddenly panic shot through her. Action without thought had been one of her sister's vices that had gotten her into more than one dilemma. Here she was doing the same thing, something she'd sworn she'd never do.

Emma groaned inwardly and bit down on her lower lip.

"He favors you."

She swung around to face a smiling Bubba. "You think so?"

"Yeah, I know so." His smile burgeoned into a full-fledged grin.

God, if only she wasn't so very conscious of him with every nerve in her body. "Thanks," she said in a slightly husky voice, "especially since he's about to be legally mine."

"That's what you told me the other day."

"He's the joy of my life."

"If you don't mind my asking, how did you end up with him?"

"He was my sister's child."

Emma hesitated, wondering if she should share her family's dirty linen with a stranger, but he seemed so harmless and most everyone in Tyler knew the truth anyway. If he didn't find out from her, he could easily find out from someone else.

"She was married at the time." After she'd said that, Emma realized her voice held a tad of defiance.

"I wasn't sitting in judgment, Emma."

Though his tone was soft and even, she heard the mockery in it, which made her feel guilty. That guilt was suddenly followed by a spurt of anger. She shouldn't care what he thought or how he reacted. But she did, and that was what bothered her. This man had managed to slip under her skin and touch her in a way that no other ever had.

And that frightened her.

Losing control of her emotions was something she couldn't allow to happen, especially not with a man with whom she had nothing in common. Nevertheless, she wasn't interested in pursuing a relationship. Her present and future resided only in Logan. She didn't see that changing.

"You got quiet all of a sudden," Bubba pointed out in a gravelly voice, his eyes trailing over her.

She wondered if he liked what he saw. Perhaps he did as she had chosen well that morning. She had on a bright coral sundress that accentuated her full breasts and hips. Her outfit was finished off with multicolored flip-flops.

Continuing to feel his gaze sweep over her, she felt a flush coming on, one that matched her dress.

"Emma?"

"I was just wondering why I should confide in you," she said in a hurried tone.

"No reason, except that I'm interested."

"Why?" she asked before she thought.

"I think you know the answer to that," he said in a low voice.

Knowing that he was intent on trapping her gaze, she swallowed hard, warning herself not to look at him, for fear of what she'd see mirrored in those often mysterious eyes—stark desire, the same desire churning within her.

"Emma, it's okay, really."

"When my sister Connie got pregnant, she filed for divorce, apparently choosing not to tell her husband about the child as he was a government agent about to leave the country." Emma shrugged. "Anyhow, to make a long, sad story short, she divorced him, then had the baby."

"Only she didn't want it."

Although Emma was taken aback by his flat statement, she didn't take offense, because it was the truth no matter how much she might want to deny it. "That's right. By then, she'd gotten involved with a biker and wanted to ride the roads with him." Emma paused and cleared her throat. "They died together in a motorcycle vehicle accident. A truck hit the motorcycle, instantly killing them both."

"I'm sorry."

"Me, too."

A silence followed during which they both watched Logan, who was still mesmerized by the other children playing on the equipment.

"He's a good baby," Cal said, breaking the tense silence.

Emma smiled with relief at the change in subject. "I think so, too. The only time he cries is when he's wet or hungry."

"That's when I cry, too."

She whipped her head up and stared at him wide-eyed. A grin covered his whole face, softening it. She grinned back. Then they both laughed out loud.

"I love to look at you," he said in a hungry tone.

Emma's grin faded instantly. She couldn't avert her eyes even though an unwanted tremor shook her body. "Don't say that. Please."

"Why not?"

"Because it's not true."

"Oh, but it is."

"My sister was the beauty in the family," Emma declared, but in a halting voice.

"Want me to start naming all your assets?"

"No," she said fiercely. Then toning down her voice, she added, "I'm sorry. I didn't mean to snap."

Cal smiled. "It's okay. Just promise me you'll look in the mirror really closely sometime."

Emma rolled her eyes. "Let's change the subject, shall we?"

"Okay, so back to the kid."

She turned and gave Logan a loving smile, then looked back at Cal but not before her smile faded. "I can hardly wait until Logan's officially mine."

"Is that in the works?" Bubba asked in a bland voice.

"Not yet, but I've been thinking seriously about setting the process in motion."

"Expecting any problems?"

She frowned. "Possibly."

"Oh?"

"His father is back in town and could cause trouble." She paused and took a deep breath. "My dad, Patrick, actually despises him. Consequently, if he does try to cause trouble, things will turn into a vicious custody fight, something I shudder to think about."

"Your father hates his ex son-in-law that much?"

She laughed without humor. "That's an understatement. He blames him for Connie's death and swears he'll kill him with his bare hands if he ever gets the chance."

"Sounds like a vindictive fellow."

Emma bristled. "Not at all. He feels that Cal Webster is scum and wouldn't be a fit father for Logan." She waited a second, then went on, "Again, Dad holds him responsible for Connie's death, which is another story I'm not prepared to go into."

"No problem."

Another silence fell between them during which Emma looked at her watch. "Mercy me, it's getting late. I best get this little bugger home and ready for bed."

"It's your call," Cal said, getting up, then staring down at her. "Can we do this again?" His gaze was deeply intense.

"What?" she asked even though she knew it was a stupid question, a stall tactic. She didn't like what was going on inside her, especially when he looked at her as if he could eat her up.

Bubba then gave her a mocking smile as though he knew exactly what she was thinking. Still, he placated her and said, "You know what. See me again."

"I…I don't know."

His eyes didn't waver. "When you make up your mind, let me know."

Before she could reply, Logan started to whimper. She was just about to reach for him when Bubba asked, "Mind?"

"Of course not, but you might want to rethink that call. He's probably soaking wet."

"Won't bother me." Cal grinned, then reached down and lifted the kid out of the stroller. Instantly, Logan started to cry.

Bubba looked so helpless that Emma giggled. "Don't take it personally. I told you he's not happy when he's wet or hungry. And right now, he's both."

"Then I suggest we haul it."

Emma reached for Logan and for a brief second, Bubba seemed reluctant to let him go. Later, she told herself she'd just imagined that.

"You got your Mommy now, kiddo. You can stop crying."

Logan grinned instantly. Both grown-ups laughed.

"I think we've just been conned," Cal said with a wink.

"No doubt," Emma agreed as she turned and headed toward his vehicle, her steps heavier than usual. If he should ask to see her again, she knew she wouldn't turn him down.

That thought sent a jolt of fear through her.

Seven

"Hey, man, why ain't we never seen you high?"

Cal cringed inwardly as the Colombian ambled closer to him, an evil gleam in his beady eyes, all the while touching the end of a needle with his grimy finger. Cal didn't so much as move a muscle. Instead, he remained cool and unruffled.

His life depended on that. Still, if he'd had his choice of torture, he'd much rather play Russian roulette with a pistol held to his head than a dirty syringe filled with cocaine jammed in his vein.

"That's because I ain't ever been high around you," Cal finally acknowledged.

The Colombian grinned an evil grin. "Well, we're about to take care of that, my friend."

Cal swallowed the urge to jump the swarthy little man and choke the very life from him. He could do that so easily because he was twice his size. But again, that was not to be, if he wanted to get out of this situation alive. The Colombian had the needle and two of his cohorts were on either side of Cal, ready to pounce should he even think about making a wrong move.

"Suit yourself," Cal said with a nonchalant shrug, though his heart was pounding with fear and dread.

The Colombian's grin widened. "Good answer, my friend. You know we can't leave you out. When you join up with us, you have to prove yourself by taking the needle."

"Go ahead and do what you gotta do," Cal responded as though he hadn't a care in the world, when in reality his fear was mounting in the form of bile in the back of his throat, threatening to choke him.

"What the hell's going on here?"

All four guys in the dank and dingy room swung around and faced the head honcho, the one that Cal had come to take down, probably one of the cruelest humans with whom he'd ever come in contact—and he'd known some nasty hombres. But this guy would have no qualms about severing your main artery and watching you bleed to death while he ate a plate full of food.

When no one uttered a word, he repeated in a low growl, "Is everyone deaf in here?"

The Colombian with the needle began to quiver. It was all Cal could do not to shout his relief out loud. However, he wasn't out of the woods yet, he reminded himself. The honcho might give this creep the go-ahead to jab him. If so, Cal figured he'd wouldn't survive. If the drugs didn't kill him, the dirty needle probably would.

"We're just about to initiate him into—"

"Not now," the boss snapped. "I have something else more pressing. All of you get your asses in gear and come with me."

The Colombian then sidled up to Cal and for his ears alone, muttered, "Your time's coming, my friend." He grinned another evil grin. "When you least expect it."

Suddenly Cal lunged upright in bed, his body covered in sweat and his stomach sour. His eyes bounced around the room while he heaved for his next breath.

When he realized he was back in the States, at his ranch, and not still in that hellhole, he went limp, then began to shake so hard his teeth banged together. Knowing it was useless to fight the effects of this nightmare, he always rode it out. Finally, his body accepted what his mind was telling him and the shaking stopped.

He felt limp, as if he'd been beaten countless times with a wet rope. After taking several more breaths, he fell back against the pillow only to grimace. It was also wet with sweat. Although uncomfortable as hell, he didn't move. Couldn't move. He was simply too exhausted.

He knew, though, that if he lay there for a while, he'd settle back to normal. This particular nightmare, and others like it, had haunted him for the duration of his undercover stint. He'd been told that it was part of the aftereffects and, in fact, to expect it.

Well, he had news for the shrinks and their advice. He might expect it, but he'd never *accept* it. He saw these mind horror shows as a weakness and he was determined to overcome them. No one was going to have that kind of power over him.

However, he was realistic enough to know that it was going to take time for him to detox, so to speak, and regain normalcy in his life. But at least he'd gotten out with his life.

There had been many times when he'd thought the breath he'd just taken was sure to be his last. There were also times when he hadn't cared a rip if that had happened. He'd become so entrenched in the seamy side of the world and the people who lived in it, he'd lost his focus and his way. No longer. He had been spared. Now he knew why.

His son.

He had a child. Imagine that. For a second Cal lay in awe, then he wanted to shout the news to the world. Realizing how ridiculous that was, he muttered out loud, "Get a grip, ol' boy. You're losing it."

He was and he wasn't.

In defense of himself, anyone who had just come through hell straight into heaven had a right to be overjoyed and proud. If only reality didn't have to be considered in the equation, he'd be home free.

Right now, reality struck with a vengeance, wreaking more havoc in his belly. What gave him the confidence to think he could be a good parent? How ludicrous was that?

Then he defended himself again. Dammit, he could learn how to parent. The child was already growing on him. Before, he'd never even thought about being a father. He and Connie had never discussed it. But then, he and Connie had never discussed anything of importance. It had been lust at first sight and hate at second sight.

A sigh filtered through Cal. Thinking ill of the dead, especially his ex-wife, made him squirm. Since day one of their marriage, he'd felt he'd made the biggest mistake of his life. Now, he wasn't so sure, not after he'd found out about the boy.

Ah, Logan.

Rearing a child was such a huge responsibility. He'd have to admit under a mental microscope that he just might not be up to the challenge, no matter how badly he might want to be. He couldn't disregard all the emotional baggage he was carrying, which included the possible backlash from his undercover work. He refused to open that closed luggage and rifle through all the dirty linen.

He had to face the fact that if he got custody of Logan, he could be putting his son in danger. Clearly that was not an option. Then he brightened. He was through with government work. He had resigned, he reminded himself; his undercover work was over.

Cal winced, remembering one particular case he had yet to bring to closure. But then that was a no-brainer and could be taken care of without endangering himself or his child.

Surely he could convince a judge of that, if it came down to a custody battle.

What about Emma?

How did *she* fit into this equation? Besides the hard, cold fact that she was the only parent Logan had ever known, he was beginning to care about her. Care, hell! He wanted to make love to her.

The evidence spoke for itself. He had only to peer down at the sheet and see his spiked manhood. When he wasn't in the throes of that horrid nightmare, he was in the throes of an erotic one—about Emma.

Since he'd first met her and perused the lushness of her body, he'd been haunted by it, wanting to see her naked, burn his eyes over her white limbs, her lush, swollen breasts, imagining how they would feel beneath his hand before he licked and sucked them.

He hadn't stopped there either. His mind had taken him deeper into that sexual adventure, an adventure that she took part in as well. He could visualize her watching him through half-closed eyes, her tongue peeping through parted lips. But it was when she moved her hips in a sensual manner, then spread her legs invitingly, that all restraints were removed.

Even in a subconscious state, he cupped her lovely buttocks and lifted them off the bed in order to have better access to that hot, wet, deliciously tight part of her. At her encouragement, he then thrust into her, feeling her muscles close around him, sweetly, while urging him on, until they both reached a hard and deep climax.

Suddenly Cal shuddered again and swung his legs over the side of the bed. When he saw that he was still hard as a brick, he muttered a curse, trudged to the bathroom and took a cold shower. Afterward, he felt better, and his head was back on straight.

Sexual intimacy with Emma Jenkins was out of the question. With the stakes so high, he had no choice but to leave his pecker in his pants and treat her for who and what she was—the stumbling block between him and his child.

In light of their previous conversation, Cal was under no illusion that he was lower than scum in her and Patrick's eyes. Without provocation or guilt, they held him accountable for Connie's death. Even though that was skewed thinking to him, that was how they saw things.

And when Emma learned his true identity, he would have the fight of his life on his hands.

Thank God, he had been forewarned.

Still, he had no intention of leaving her alone. That wasn't an option either. He continued to have hope that by endearing himself to her, he would soften her to the point that they could work something out concerning Logan, thus keeping the battle out of the courts.

Cal winced again, thinking he had probably nixed any form of civility from the get-go, having blatantly lied to Emma about his true identity. Shoving aside another severe pang of guilt, he dressed with haste.

When he climbed into his truck later, he knew where he was headed. Despite that insanity, he couldn't wait.

"Am I ever glad to see you."

Patrick grinned at Emma, then leaned over and kissed her lightly on the cheek. "What's wrong, honey?"

Emma rolled her eyes over to Logan who was swinging in his electric swing, gnawing on a rubber toy. It was obvious he'd been crying as there were streaks of dried tears on his cheeks.

"Uh-oh, the little fellow's been on a roll."

"That's an understatement," Emma said, following a sigh. "He literally pitched a hissy fit. Went stiff as a board. The whole nine yards, actually."

"About what?"

"Does he have to have a reason?" Emma heard the exasperation in her voice, but made no apologies for it. She often wondered, as she did today, if she were cut out to be a mother. Then her self-confidence would kick in when she thought of the alternative. She could never give Logan up, no matter what.

He was hers.

"Hey, how 'bout if I take him for a while?"

"Oh, Daddy, that would be such a help. With Janet off sick, I'm swamped."

Patrick frowned. "Why don't you hire more help? You can certainly afford it."

"It's not that."

"Then what is it? It's obvious you want to spend more time with Logan."

"You're right about that." Emma thrust her hands through her hair, mussing it up a bit more. "I just can't seem to leave him for long."

"And that's not a bad thing, my dear. It's all the reason to hire more help."

"Perhaps I'll give that some serious thought," Emma said with a smile that quickly faded. "You haven't heard anything more about Cal Webster being back in the area, have you?"

Patrick's mouth twisted. "No, but I'm seriously thinking about hiring a detective to check it out—check *him* out."

"I'm not sure I want to know if he's around or not."

"Then I won't tell you."

Emma's eyes widened. "You can't do that."

Patrick's lips twitched. "You can't have it both ways."

"I suppose not," Emma responded, down in the mouth.

"Look, let's not worry about that right now," Patrick said in a cajoling tone. "Or anytime, for that matter. I've already told you, Webster's not getting near that boy. You'll just have to trust me on that."

"I do," Emma responded with a smile. "Look, since he's asleep, I'll just keep him."

Patrick frowned. "Are you sure? You know I don't mind watching him."

"I know, Daddy, and I appreciate it, but when he's awakened, he's grumpier than ever."

"I'll take your word for it," Patrick said with a smile.

Emma looked on as he strode over to the swing and lightly kissed the cheek of the still-sleeping baby. Then, winking at her, Patrick turned and made his way to his truck.

She was still smiling an hour later when she heard what sounded like a truck pull up in front of the shop. When she went to the front and looked out, her heart lurched. Bubba was just slamming the truck door. He saw her and pulled up short.

For a long moment, their eyes met and held. Then he sauntered towards her, sending her pulse rate skyrocketing. Why did he always have to look so damn sexy? *Be* so damn sexy?

She didn't want to be attracted to him. Only she was, and couldn't deny it. When he came within sight, her body did strange things. Today was no different. He was dressed in a worn shirt that showed off his muscles to perfection and a pair of tight-fitting jeans that left no doubt that he was well-hung.

Where had that thought come from? After shaking her head to clear it, Emma said, "I'm not due a delivery today."

"I know," he said, while his eyes roamed her body.

She felt a flush creep into her face. "Then why are you here?"

"I think you know."

Emma swallowed hard. "No, I don't."

"Yes, you do." His voice grew huskier. "But I don't mind saying it. I came to see you."

"I don't think that's a good idea."

"You're probably right."

Taken aback by his agreement, she blinked hard.

He smiled. "But that doesn't mean I'm leaving."

"Bubba—"

"What, Emma?" he asked in a teasing voice.

"You know what," she responded, though with little conviction.

"How 'bout having dinner with me?"

"I can't."

"Why not?"

"I have Logan."

"Not a problem. He can come, too."

"You don't understand."

"Suppose you enlighten me."

"Bubba," she said with uncensored exasperation.

"Emma," he mocked, then added, "Please."

She bit down on her lower lip and knew what she was about to say would be tantamount to another trip down Suicide Lane. "All right. But you come to my place, and I'll make dinner."

Eight

She had done it again.

Emma had followed her heart instead of her common sense. Hence, she was in a real funk. However, she had no one to blame but herself. She had gone to great efforts to get the house in order in preparation for his visit. Not that anything was really dirty or out of place—it wasn't.

Her scurrying around, doing busy work, was more for her own good than anything else. When her hands were occupied, she usually didn't beat up on herself as much. Not so this evening.

Dammit, she didn't want to be attracted to Bubba or Bart—whatever the hell his name was. Nothing had changed on that score. When he'd suggested getting together, she'd jumped on the invitation without a rational thought.

In reality, she'd like to jump on *him*.

A horrifying shudder tore through Emma. Glory be!

How could she let her mind keep dwelling on the chemistry that flared between them? Because she wanted him. Apparently that need was what had precipitated this latest foolhardy deed.

After she'd blurted out the invitation, the air had literally throbbed with tension. Bubba seemed caught off guard, and she wondered just how much deeper she was going to dig her own hole before sound judgment returned. Dear Lord, she hadn't wanted to spend the evening with him. So why hadn't she kept her mouth shut?

"That's fine with me," he'd responded, a vein beating in his neck.

Instead of looking at him, she had watched his Adam's apple bob up and down. "Are you sure?" she asked in a low voice.

"More than sure." His gaze trapped hers. "Can I bring anything?"

"Uh, no." She licked her lips. "Just yourself."

"I wouldn't do that, if I were you."

"What?" she asked, hearing the catch in her voice, sounding like a hiccup.

"Lick your lips."

"Oh." That was all she could manage to say.

Humor lit his eyes, then his lips quirked into an incredibly sexy grin. "I like your style, Emma Jenkins."

Feeling more confused than ever, she quickly averted her gaze, fearful of what he'd see in her eyes.

"Are you sure I can't bring anything? Wine or beer?"

"I have both," she said, glad the air was no longer vibrating with a heavy sexual tension.

"Can't beat a deal like that." Bubba's grin widened.

She didn't respond. *Couldn't*. That grin of his had her tongue-tied like a teenager on her first date.

"I'll see you at—"

He left the sentence unfinished, which forced her gaze back on him. His eyes probed. Ignoring the banked-down fire she saw in them, Emma said, "Sevenish."

Now, as she continued to putter around the house, readying herself for his arrival, she realized she was expending good energy for nothing. Muttering a foul word, she tossed the dusting rag.

In that instant the phone rang. Maybe it was Bubba calling to cancel, she told herself, brightening. But when she looked at caller ID and saw that it wasn't him, she felt a sense of relief.

"Hey, Dad, what's up?"

"Food."

"Food?"

"I'm out and about and just bought more Chinese than I can eat. I know how much you like it, so how 'bout I share?"

"Now?" she asked, experiencing panic of a different kind.

Patrick chuckled. "What kind of question is that, girl? Of course, now."

"It's not a good time," Emma declared off the top of her head and then knew that was a mistake. He would demand an explanation, which meant she'd have to tell an untruth. No way was she prepared to share her interest in a man with her daddy. Besides, her infatuation with Bubba was only that—an infatuation that would soon pass. To make a big deal out of it would be stupid, upsetting Patrick for no reason.

He'd often encouraged her to go out with men, but she

wasn't convinced he meant it. He liked being the only father figure in his grandson's life, and she was willing to bet if she did find a significant other, he wouldn't be happy.

"Look, Daddy, I'm tired and Logan's still fussy."

He didn't say anything.

"I'm sorry." She groped hard to find something soothing to say. "I hope I didn't hurt your feelings," she added lamely.

"You didn't," Patrick responded in a puzzled tone.

She could visualize him scratching his head, as if trying to figure out what was going on with her since she rarely had any objections to his impromptu visits.

"I'll talk to you tomorrow, okay?"

A silence fell over the line, during which Emma held her breath.

"Whatever."

Patrick hung up then, and Emma let go of her pent-up breath. But she knew he was far from happy. And most curious. While she would've loved to have him stop by, she dared not chance it. Time was close at hand.

At least she had the meal prepared, though it was certainly nothing fancy. According to her father, chicken salad was her forte. She'd whipped up a batch last evening because she'd been restless. That was what she was serving along with croissants, a plate of fresh tomatoes, dip and chips. For dessert, she'd picked up a dozen cranberry-orange tea cakes from a bakery.

Emma was on her way to the bedroom when she stopped in her tracks, hearing a whine through the baby monitor. She dashed into Logan's room and lifted him out of his Pac 'n Play. "What's the matter, little fellow?"

"Mama," he said, wrapping his chubby arms around her neck and placing his head on her shoulder.

Emma heard his breathing calm instantly as she rubbed his back. "Were you having a bad dream, darling?"

Logan merely clung tighter.

She glanced at her watch and saw that it was almost time for Bubba to get there. But wild horses wouldn't make her desert her baby even though she needed to repair her makeup and change her clothes. If he saw her dressed in skimpy shorts, T-shirt and very little makeup, then so be it. She wasn't trying to impress him.

Or was she?

Unwilling to answer that question, along with others that circulated through her brain, Emma sat down and began to rock Logan. But he didn't instantly fall back to sleep as he did most other times. Twice she tried to put him down, and he started whimpering again, clinging tighter. Her only recourse was to rock him some more.

"It's okay, baby," she whispered against his tiny ear. "Mommy's not going to let you go."

And she wasn't. Not ever. It was all she could do not to squeeze him until he cried out, as thoughts of Logan's father flashed through her mind. Since Patrick had told her that Cal Webster was in the area, she'd often had this same vision, sometimes at night and sometimes during the day. In it Cal would sneak into her home and whisk her child out of her arms—*out of her life.*

She wished she knew what he looked like. Actually, she'd never been curious, since the marriage had been a big mistake from the get-go and hadn't lasted. But now, she regretted that. Maybe tomorrow she'd ask her daddy for a description of Webster so she'd be armed. Just in case.

When that kind of irrational thinking hit her, Emma panicked. That panic was always followed by an adrenaline flow that sent her running to the bathroom in a cold sweat. Thankfully, the reality of clutching Logan in her arms shot down that panic and kept her rational.

Finally, Logan went back to sleep. With cautious care, she placed him once again into his Pac 'n Play. After watching him breathe for perhaps a minute, she smiled, thinking he was soon going to outgrow that fancy play pen and graduate into a real bed.

That made her sad. She didn't want him to grow up so fast. She loved him depending on her for everything. Soon he'd be wanting to do things on his own, without her help. Following a resigned sigh, Emma tiptoed out, closing the door softly behind her. The baby monitors would keep her apprised of any need that might arise.

Emma had just managed to brush her teeth and slap on a bit of lip gloss when the doorbell rang. She took a deep, lung-expanding breath, trying to stave off the erratic beat of her heart. By the time she reached the door, she had to force herself not to think about how hard her nipples were pressing against her T-shirt.

She flung open the door and his blue eyes instantly locked with hers.

"Hey," Bubba said in a ragged voice, his gaze dropping instantly to her mouth.

"Hey, yourself," she barely managed to answer.

Bubba remained propped against a pillar on her porch, his tanned features disturbingly sensual. Like her, he had on shorts and a T-shirt that again left no doubt as to the shape and size of his muscles, especially his biceps. Just looking at him turned her inside out.

Damn, what kind of hold did this man have on her?

"Come in," she said at last, expelling a breath.

Sudden humor settled in the deep grooves of his eyes. "Thanks."

He didn't face her again until he was deep into her living area. "Mmm, nice."

"I…we enjoy it."

"Speaking of we, where is that chunk of lead?"

Although she'd never heard that expression, she thought it fit Logan. She smiled. "He's sleeping, though I expect that to change at any moment. It's almost feeding time."

"Good."

She didn't respond to that, not really knowing how. He seemed to have taken a liking to Logan. For all she knew, he felt that way about all kids. She had no idea, reminding herself how little she knew about this man and his personal life.

If she should continue to see him, maybe that should change. He knew far more about her than she did about him, which wasn't fair.

"Would you like something to drink?" she asked, breaking into the suddenly awkward silence.

"A beer."

"Have a seat, and I'll be right back."

"Need any help?"

"No, thanks."

"Hurry back."

That urgent tone almost pulled her up short. Then, regaining control of her fractured emotions, Emma strode into the kitchen where she leaned heavily against the counter.

This had to stop, she chastised herself. Her reaction to

this man was crazy. Maybe she ought to take the bull by the horns, so to speak, pull his head down and kiss the fire out of him. Then maybe she could get him out of her system.

Wonder what he'd think about that?

With cheeks the color of scarlet, Emma hurried about the business of getting the drinks. Once they were on a tray, she made her way back to the great room. He was standing in front of the big expanse of glass that showed off her small but perfectly groomed backyard.

He turned around. "If your other jobs are anything like this, you're one hell of a landscaper."

His compliment took her slightly aback. "Well, thanks."

"You're welcome," he said in a mocking tone, his eyes once again dropping to her lips, even as he moved closer.

In spite of herself, Emma quivered and wanted to step back, fearing his nearness. But sheer will forced her not to move, unwilling to let him know the profound effect he had on her.

The scent that was so him—clean and manly— swamped her senses. If she so much as closed her eyes, she knew what would happen. She'd sway into him with water-like limbs.

That couldn't happen. Only it did. Unconsciously, she must have drifted, because strong fingers wrapped around her bare forearms, sending an electric shock through her system.

Emma's eyes opened, and she gasped. His features swam before her eyes. "I—what about our drinks?" she stammered, trying desperately to squelch the tension that held them in its grips.

"Forget them," he rasped, allowing the back of his knuckles to trail down one cheek. "You don't have anything on under that shirt, do you?"

Her mouth parted on another gasp, which apparently played right into his plans as his middle finger brushed across her bottom lip, back and forth.

"Aren't you going to answer me?"

He knew damn well she couldn't answer him. He knew what he was doing to her. She could see it in his eyes, in the glint that narrowed them. "Yes...no," she finally admitted out of desperation.

He gave her an indulgent smile. "Whatever you say."

Almost involuntarily, her hands splayed across his chest. She told herself later that she'd touched him with the intention of pushing him away. But about that time, he increased the probing of her lip, leaving her feeling weak, drained and unresistant.

From that moment on, she couldn't think of anything, or feel anything but him and what he was doing to her body. The consequences of her actions were not important. As if surprised at her acquiescence, Bubba muttered something sounding much like a moan, then replaced his finger with his mouth.

Though it was just a surface kiss, it packed the voltage of shock akin to a bolt of lightning striking her. Her lips opened willingly as his tongue flicked across hers, igniting more sparks. Lust, hot and complete, thundered through her veins, threatening to consume her.

Even the distant sound of warning bells clanging in her head failed to stop her hands from winding around his neck, deepening the kiss, playing the seductress. That was when it hit her just how irresistibly powerful the pull of lust could be.

Nothing mattered except the fire now raging through her, ending up between her legs, causing an ache that was both unfamiliar and exhilarating. Her stomach clinched and her whole body felt alive and hot with an unfulfilled need. Her eyes closed without provocation. For the first time ever she realized what it meant to really want a man. It was a sensation she didn't ever want to end.

Only it did. He ended it.

With a muttered curse against her lips, Bubba dug his fingers deeper into her flesh and, stopping just short of hurting her, he created a distance between them.

"This is crazy," he muttered, his voice so thick it seemed to slur.

Mortified, Emma sucked in her breath then began to shake. Oh dear Lord, she was doing exactly what she'd sworn never to do—she was behaving like her sister. She lusted after a stranger, reveled in the feel of his arms and lips.

Heaven help her.

Nine

"Do you want me to leave?" Bubba's features were tight and his voice low. "It's your call."

Emma folded her arms across her chest as if that gesture would stop her quivering insides. Of course, she wanted him to go. Only she didn't. It seemed that he was having more trouble coming to grips with the hot kiss than she was, which added to her humiliation.

Did he have something to hide, some dark secret that plagued him? What if he'd lied about being divorced? What if he had a record or something awful like that? What if…?

She slammed her mind shut, unwilling to travel that destructive path, at least not right now.

"Emma," he said harshly.

She had to lick her lips moist before she could utter a word. "What do you want to do?"

"What do *you* want me to do?" That harsh edge remained in his voice.

She chanced a look at him. His face was drawn, and she could see a muscle twitching in his jaw, another indication he wasn't as calm as he appeared.

"It's not really my decision, is it?" After all, he'd been the one to pull away, much to her horror. She hadn't been strong enough.

"Isn't it?"

"Can we forget—" Her voice failed, and she stared up at him helplessly.

"That we made love with our lips?"

She gasped at his bluntness. "Is…that what we did?"

"You tell me." His voice had dropped to a lower pitch.

Oh, God, he was mesmerizing her again. But this time she wouldn't give in. "I've never done anything like this before."

"Like what?"

He seemed to enjoy tormenting her because that was exactly what he was doing. "Kissing someone I don't know."

"A stranger, you mean?"

"Exactly," she said with emphasis.

His eyes delved. "I thought we'd gotten to know each other pretty well."

"There's still a lot I don't know about you."

"Such as?"

"Why you're driving a plant truck." Emma almost bit her tongue. Where had that come from? That had sounded so inane, so out of place, so unlike her.

If he was taken aback by her words, he didn't show it. Actually, he smiled, that slow smile that had the power to heat her insides like a furnace. "I'm just doing that until I find more security work."

"When you grow up, huh?"

He laughed outright. "Exactly."

The silence that fell between them simmered with added sexual tension.

He ended it by saying in a breaking voice, "I want to stay."

"Then stay," she said.

"Only keep my hands to myself?"

"I think that would be wise," she said, averting her gaze.

"You got it."

Suddenly she heard Logan whimper. "Look, I have to see about the baby. I'll be right back."

Once she made it to the nursery, she leaned over the bed. But before she picked up Logan, she had to get her head on straight and her breathing leveled out. She couldn't face Bubba in this shape, though she knew she hadn't done anything wrong.

A feeling of acute despair suddenly washed over Emma, the image of her sister very much in front of her. But again, she had to put things in perspective and call a spade a spade. She liked this man and had wanted him to kiss her, which in itself was mind-boggling, making her second-guess herself.

Before he appeared in her life—out of the blue—she had been content without a man. Now, she wasn't so sure. Bubba had stirred something inside her she hadn't known existed.

The scary part was that the unknown emotion threatened to take precedence over everything else. Logan *was* the issue here, not her. Her reputation had to remain spotless and her mind focused if she were going to qualify as a parent rather than just as a legal guardian. She didn't want anything to jeopardize that.

Ergo, getting involved with a man now would not be a smart move. It was time she thought seriously about filing for custody of Logan, especially with Cal Webster lurking about. Once he was located, she hoped he would sign the necessary papers relinquishing his parental rights. That done, she could then file for adoption and become Logan's legal parent. Then she would be assured of never losing him.

The thought that Webster might not be receptive to that plan didn't enter her mind. It couldn't, for fear of what it would do to her emotionally and mentally. She couldn't quite control that constant niggling in the back of her mind that her plan might indeed backfire.

A hard shudder knifed through her.

"Mama," Logan cried again, jerking her back to the moment at hand. He was standing, his chubby fingers embedded in the material of her T-shirt.

"Sorry, sweetheart," she murmured, lifting him into her arms.

"I hope you don't mind—"

On hearing Bubba's voice, Emma whipped around so fast she knew she'd robbed him of the rest of his sentence. He looked startled.

"I was afraid you hadn't heard me," he said by way of explanation.

"That's okay," she responded, feeling her heart rate almost settle back to normal.

"Is the little fellow okay?"

Emma gave him a wobbly smile, still unsure of how the remainder of the evening would play out, that kiss uppermost in her mind. His hot and passionate eyes seemed to eat her up.

"Logan's fine," she said with a nervous laugh. "He's just hungry."

"So am I." He smiled, then winked. "But that growing boy comes first."

"You're right about that," she said in a strong tone.

"Mind if I watch you feed him?"

"Not in the least," she said, moving toward the door with Logan balanced on her hip. It wouldn't matter if she had, she told herself. When she'd told Bubba he could stay, she'd made a commitment. As long as she kept her emotions out of it, she could get through the rest of the evening without anything else happening.

"He's a chunk of change, isn't he?"

Emma ruffled Logan's dark curls. "That he is."

"Man," Logan said, pointing at Cal.

Emma watched as Bubba reached out and caught hold of that finger and gently pulled it. "Smart kid."

Logan grinned at him, then hid his face against Emma's chest.

"I think he likes you."

"Would you mind if I held him?"

"He probably won't let you."

Cal's mouth curved downward. "You're probably right. It's too soon." He tousled Logan's hair. "Maybe next time, huh?"

The baby merely grinned at him again when Emma said, "Mommy's going to feed her baby."

"Baby," Logan mimicked.

A few minutes later she was spooning food into Logan's mouth, ever mindful of Bubba's big body sitting beside her watching her every move.

"You're really good with him."

Emma flashed a spontaneous smile, but refused to meet his penetrating gaze. She simply didn't trust herself. "You really think so?"

"Yeah, I think so," he said in a slow drawl.

That drawl hiked her pulse but she didn't let on. She just kept shoveling food into Logan's mouth.

"So what happens next?" he asked, lightening the building tension.

"With Logan, you mean?"

"Yep."

"Bath, then bed."

"That sounds logical."

Emma looked at him this time, feeling a smile rearrange her lips. "Want to watch the bath, too?"

"You bet. Wouldn't miss that for anything."

"I'm sorry we can't eat now. I know you're starving. Maybe you should drink your beer, though I'm sure it's tepid." Why did she care if he had anything to eat or drink? She didn't owe him an apology for not feeding him. She didn't owe him *anything*.

"Ah, forget about me," he said lightly. "I'm just fine while I'm watching you. Feed the boy, that is."

Emma cast him a look before concentrating once again on the task before her. Shortly, she was finished, but not before the baby and everything around him was smeared with peas and stewed peaches.

"You're a mess, kiddo," Cal said, reaching out and touching his forearm.

Logan merely grinned and kicked his feet.

"Whoa, boy." Emma chuckled. "Those feet of yours could turn into lethal weapons, especially if you hit Mommy with them."

Logan's feet kicked harder.

Emma stood just in time. Holding his feet, she removed the high-chair tray, then swooped Logan into her arms. "Whew, stinky boy," she said, wiping his mouth and face. "You really need a bath."

"You think he'd let me hold him now?" Cal asked, "While you draw his water."

"I guess we could give it a try." She didn't know why she was reluctant to let Bubba hold Logan. Maybe the reason was so simple she was missing it. Maybe it was because she didn't want to share him with anyone. But then that wasn't true. She shared him with her dad all the time. So what was the difference?

She knew the answer without delving too far into her subconscious. It was her own insecurities when it came to men. She'd never been willing to share herself with anyone, let another soul get this close to her. Fears resulting from her sister's behavior had forced her to erect a wall around her heart.

The fact that this man, now reaching for her baby, had managed to chip away at that wall didn't set well with her. She and Logan were a team unto themselves. At this point in their lives, they didn't need any other players.

"All right," Cal said, holding Logan in the air when he showed signs of tearing up.

"Careful, he's just eaten. He's liable to empty the contents of his tummy on you."

Cal's hands froze in midair. When he looked down at her, she saw pure panic and laughed.

"You're just jerking my chain," he said, resuming his jostling of the child.

About that time, Logan's tummy gurgled then let go of

a big glob of baby food that landed with a splat square in the middle of Cal's forehead.

Bubba's eyes riveted to hers, a horrified look on his face. She stared back at him with a look that said, told you so.

Then they both started laughing and didn't stop until their sides hurt.

Ten

Cal was sweating like a pig.

What did he expect? He'd been mending fences all morning, which was certainly no piece of cake. He paused, removed his hat and swiped his forehead with a red bandana he'd stuffed in the back pocket of his jeans. If he was perspiring like this now, he wondered what kind of summer they were in store for.

He took several deep breaths when his chest constricted unexpectedly. Maybe his reaction to hard labor and the climate resulted from him being cooped up for the past year.

God, he'd hated that, hated being behind closed doors. More times than not, he'd questioned his choice of careers, thinking he'd have been better served if he'd become a forester so that he could stomp through the woods and get paid for it.

No point in traveling down that road, he told himself.

It would only lead to a dead end. He reined in his mind as he walked to the huge oak tree where he got a sip of water from his cooler.

His foreman had helped early on, but as the day turned warmer, he'd told Art to take the rest of the day off and go home, that he'd worked long enough.

Cal, however, hadn't stopped. It was important to finish the project—he never started something he didn't finish; that went against his grain. He realized he was pushing himself past his limits. He was feeding his fetish for punishing his mind and body.

Last night was the culprit.

His chest constricted again and it wasn't from the heat. He was playing one more deadly and dangerous game. This time it wasn't with strangers either. It was with people he cared about, which upped the stakes even more.

Actually Emma was the culprit.

In the short time he'd known her he'd become obsessed with her. Another pang of guilt suddenly whopped him upside the head. Since he'd met her, he hadn't been able to get her off his mind. Everywhere he went, she went with him. Everything he did, she did it with him. If that wasn't obsession, he didn't know what it was.

"Shit," he muttered, swiping his forehead once again.

A cluster of birds perched on a branch above him began to chirp in unison as though answering him. Any other time, he would've smiled, a contentment washing through him, thinking he had it made. He was out of confinement, back on his ranch, doing what he loved doing.

How he'd longed for this time. While undercover, dealing with the drug kingpins, he had thought of tasting the clean air, feeling the breeze on his skin and hearing the birds.

Like now.

Only now he couldn't concentrate on the magic of the ranch or anything else. He simply couldn't empty his mind of Emma and the web she had woven over him. The urge to taste her lips again stabbed at him like a dull knife, deep into his core being, not to mention the tight feeling it created in his jeans. From the first minute he had seen her, he'd wanted her.

He'd tried every tactic in the book to downplay his ever-growing desire for her, realizing that she could do things to him that neither her sister nor any other woman had ever done.

That hadn't changed.

He knew, however, that no matter how tempting she might be, he had to keep his distance. He couldn't keep on thinking about her, dreaming about her, aching to taste her.

She was forbidden fruit. At least until the custody issue was settled. And rightly so, too. The thought of what she would do, how she would react, especially in light of the other night's fiasco, didn't bear thinking about. The only thing on his mind was that ever-tightening web of deceit.

After he'd lied to her about his identity, *in hindsight, a suicidal idea,* it hadn't taken him long to realize he'd screwed up royally. Now it was too late. She'd snared him, and he had no desire to untangle himself.

Especially not after he'd kissed her again.

A groan of conscience carried Cal's mind back to the second when that wet glob of food had landed on his face, and they had doubled over with laughter. What happened after that had rocked his world.

And still did.

Following that bout of laughter, their gazes had caught

and held. During that long moment, Cal could barely breathe. It was as though his lung capacity had shut down, making another breath impossible.

"We'd better clean you up," Emma had said, *her* breathing not quite right either.

Still, neither moved. Every nerve in his body had rebelled against losing that moment, but he'd finally cleared his throat hard and said, "Whatever you say."

Logan was not about to be ignored, anyway. He started pulling on Emma's nose and putting his hands in her mouth.

"No, no," she said, catching his hands in hers. "It's time to put you in the bathtub."

He smiled. "Maybe I should join Logan, since I probably stink as well."

She returned his smile, then said, "You don't stink now, but you will if you don't wash your face."

He had followed her into the bathroom, all the while admiring the way her cute, tight ass filled those cutoffs. It was all he could do to refrain from reaching out, grabbing one of those cheeks. In order to refrain, Cal had fallen slightly behind, curling his fingers into his palms.

While Emma drew the baby's bathwater, he cleaned himself up with a cloth she gave him. Once that was done, Logan was in the tub with her squatted beside it. Cal looked on in amusement as he knelt beside her, careful not to get too close.

As it was, the clean, slightly exotic smell of her threatened to overwhelm his senses. He couldn't take his eyes off her while she splashed water over the baby, who had a rubber toy stuffed in his mouth. His fingers itched to caress Emma's exposed cheek, to take advantage of this unexpected intimacy. How would she react if he decided to test the waters?

He wasn't going to find out.

"Look, you little rascal," Emma said, laughing, "Mommy needs to wash you, then you can play."

Logan merely grinned at her and kept on splashing.

"You'd best move back." Her gaze sought his. "Or you're liable to get drenched.

He chuckled. "That wouldn't be the worse thing that ever happened to me."

"I guess not, not after getting missiled with a glob of baby food," she responded, with a smile altering her full lips.

"As you can see, I survived it." He heard the huskiness in his voice and cleared it.

Emma turned her gaze back on Logan, as though afraid their eyes might lock again. If only she didn't have the power to kick him in the gut with her every move. *Downright sexy* were the only words to describe her. Perhaps that was because she was more voluptuous than any woman he'd ever been interested in.

Unlike her sibling, Emma wasn't thin. Her breasts, while certainly perky, were rather large for her frame— more than a mouthful, that was for sure. And her hips and buttocks—well, their fullness already had him salivating.

Only the baby's presence prevented him from doing the outrageous and that was to reach out, grab her chin, and turn her face so that he could kiss those succulent lips until she cried out for mercy.

Cal expelled a weary breath about the time Emma yelped, "Logan, stop it."

He whipped his head around just in time to get a face full of soapy water.

Although he didn't open his eyes for a long moment, he heard Emma suck in her breath, then burst into giggles. "Oh, Logan, you bad boy. See what you did."

Slowly, and feeling an answering grin creep across his lips, Cal wiped his eyes, then opened them. Emma's giggles had dried up and while circling an arm tightly around the baby, she stared at Cal wide-eyed, her glossy lips parted. "I—"

He groaned, then did the unthinkable. He lowered his head and sank his lips onto hers. They both seemed to freeze, then with a groan coming from deep within, he thrust his tongue inside her mouth. This time, she groaned as the kiss turned hotter, deeper, becoming a sensual invasion.

Instantly, the tightening in his groin turned painful as his hand circled one full breast, then the other, kneading each until the engorged nipples pushed into his palm, seeming to scorch his skin.

Finding no resistance, Cal matched wits with her tongue in an erotic sparring match, envisioning them naked on the floor, thrashing about, limbs entwined, before he plunged his manhood hard and high into her honey hole.

Lust thundered through his veins, holding him captive by the unfulfilled cravings of his body.

It was Logan, again, who called a halt to the moment's madness. He let out a happy squeal that forced Cal to drag his lips away. Both swung around to face the baby, their breathing way out of whack.

"Logan, what's—"

Cal heard the thickness in her voice, reminding him of a rich cream, making him go hard again.

Logan answered her with a grin as if to say he didn't like being ignored.

"Is that his modus operandi for getting attention?" Cal asked, his breathing slightly accelerated.

"Seems so," she responded, still without looking at him.

A silence fell between them as he continued to stare at her profile, wondering if he'd cut his own throat by his actions. He didn't have long to find out.

"Look, I think it's best you leave," she said in a shaky voice.

"You're probably right."

Another silence.

"Look at me, Emma."

"I don't want to."

For a second, her response reminded him of an errant child. He blew out his breath. "I don't intend to leave you alone."

"Please, just go."

He didn't argue with her. Instead he did her bidding, only to realize when he got in his truck that he never did get anything to eat. Didn't matter, he told himself. He couldn't have digested it anyway. As the evening ended, all he wanted was to get dog-sucking drunk.

Suddenly a buzzing around Cal's head jerked him back to stark reality. Realizing the culprit was a red wasp, he dodged, then stepped out of harm's way. Making a face, his gaze whipped to the sagging fence.

"Aw, to hell with it," he muttered harshly.

He might as well call it quits for the day. Rehashing the situation was not only painful but a waste of time. What was done was done. Anyway, he was exhausted. But he knew he wouldn't rest. Crazy or not, he'd shower, then do what he had to do.

He'd go see his son. And Emma.

Logan.

Heretofore, his mind had been camped on Emma. But he was equally as smitten with his child, only in a different way, of course. He'd never been around babies much, never having felt the need for that kind of responsibility, much less that kind of bond.

Maybe he'd always been too selfish. Whatever the reason, his past feelings no longer counted. The boy was delightful, creating a desperate desire within him to become a vital and integral part of Logan's life. That desire was fast becoming a festering ache, akin to the one he felt for Emma.

However, Logan was his flesh and blood, but was off limits to him. That smarted, which left Cal no alternative but to stay the course.

Yep, he'd made the commitment to walk this wounding path, and he had no choice but to complete the journey. But that didn't mean he had to like it. It was just something he had to do.

Or at least try. Gathering his tools, he made his way back to the house, his steps more determined than ever.

"How much more dirt can that kid eat?"

Emma rolled her eyes. "Logan, stop that. This minute."

Cal chuckled. "Methinks you're talking to hear your head rattle."

Emma doubted that because she questioned whether she had anything in her head to rattle. After all, she had agreed to see Bubba again, consenting to let him take her and Logan to the park where the baby had been playing for over an hour now.

Swallowing a sigh, she reached for Logan, then wiped the dirt off his mouth and hands. For a moment thereafter, he was content to let her hold him. She hoped he would fall asleep.

"What are you thinking about?"

"Wishing Logan would go to sleep."

If Bubba was disappointed in her response, he didn't show it. He merely grinned. "Good luck in getting that to happen."

"It's going to take more than luck. It's going to take a miracle."

This time he threw back his head and laughed outright, which caused Emma's breath to catch. Then, adding insult to injury, he winked at her.

Before he could read the fire that was sure to have leapt into her eyes, she looked down at Logan.

"You can run but you can't hide," Bubba said in a raspy tone.

"I don't know what you mean."

"Sure you do," he drawled.

Don't, she told herself. Don't succumb to that sexual charisma. Twice now, he'd kissed her. If she didn't watch herself, there would be a third incident, and on and on they would go.

She still didn't know why she couldn't shake the hold he had over her, but she couldn't. To make matters worse, here she was at the park with him, aware of him with every nerve in her body. Did she think anything good was going to come of her fascination with this man? Of course not. He was just passing through her life.

Maybe she shouldn't be satisfied with kisses. Maybe she

should go ahead and have a passionate love affair with him. Maybe she'd get him out of her system, thus returning her life back to normal. While he intrigued and excited her, certainly sexually, there could be no future because she didn't want one, especially not with a man who remained a mystery.

All the more reason *not* to have sex with him.

"You look pretty today," he said in that same raspy tone.

Before she thought, Emma looked up and around, straight into those vivid blue eyes. Though his gaze was roaming unabashedly over her, thank heavens those killer dimples were nowhere to be seen. That would have been more than her heart could've stood. Even now it was going bonkers inside her chest.

Would this madness ever end?

"Uh, thank you," she said, flushing.

She hadn't intended to look special. She had chosen a pair of low-rise, pink capris, the hems stitched in sparkly beads, and a matching cropped top that left her tanned midriff, including her naval, open for inspection.

His inspection, she thought with a gulp.

"You're welcome." His tone mocked while his lips twitched.

Unable to cope with the mounting sexual attraction that danced between them, Emma rose and stood Logan on the ground. Immediately he trotted off and she followed.

It happened so suddenly that in retrospect she still couldn't believe it. In a matter of seconds, Logan fell down and then let out a howl.

"Oh, baby," Emma cried, bending down.

That was when she saw the blood streaming from his

eyebrow. She froze, while her stomach turned a somersault.

"What's wrong?" Cal demanded, kneeling on the other side of Logan. Before she could get anything through her closed throat, he snatched up the child. "Come on, let's go."

Twenty minutes later found them in the E.R., sitting in the waiting room, Cal's handkerchief over the wound, stopping the flow of blood.

"It's okay, darling," she whispered against Logan's ears, trying to calm his whimpers, beating up on herself for not seeing the fall coming. If she hadn't been so caught up in thinking about Bubba, this wouldn't have happened. She blamed herself, which made her nauseous. Knowing she was about to be sick, she shifted Logan onto Bubba's lap.

Shock filled his eyes.

"I'm sick. I'll be right back." She scurried to the bathroom where she promptly lost the contents of her stomach. It was after she'd rinsed her mouth and patted her face with cold water that she reached for the cell phone stashed in her pocket.

When she made her way back into the waiting room, Logan was howling.

"Are you all right?" Cal asked, handing the baby to her.

"I'm fine."

He made a face. "Couldn't prove it by me."

She didn't bother to acknowledge that. Instead she said, "What's taking them so long?"

"We should be next," Cal said in a confident voice, holding his bandana against the wound.

"Do you think he'll have to get stitches?"

"Probably not."

She wilted with relief. "The thought of a needle piercing Logan's tender skin makes me sick to my stomach again."

Bubba opened his mouth, only to slam it shut, a strange expression appearing on his face. She tracked his eyes and watched as her father hurried into the waiting area.

Emma stood with a muted cry. "Thank God, you're here."

"Is this some kind of joke?" Patrick demanded in a voice that clearly shook with rage.

Emma felt all the color drain from her face, noticing that her dad's eyes were narrowed on Bubba, who was now standing.

Her gaze bounced between them, finally landing back on Patrick and staying there. "I hardly think a split in my son's head is a joke."

"I'm not talking about Logan," Patrick spat. "I'm talking about this scumbag you're with."

Emma licked her dry lips, groping to understand what was going on.

"Dammit, girl, have you gone daft?"

"Do you know something about Bubba that I don't know?"

"Bubba, hell." Patrick's voice shook with rage. "This is none other than your sister's ex-husband, Cal Webster."

Eleven

Horror gripped her.

Then a combination of dizziness and nausea set in.

"Dammit, Emma," Patrick said, dashing to her side and grasping her arm. "Don't you dare faint on me. This s.o.b. isn't worth that."

Her dad's harsh words miraculously did the trick. Emma rallied herself both mentally and physically. Although shriveling up on the inside, she clutched her child to her, then stared at her ex brother-in-law, a grim look plastered on his face.

"How dare you?" she said in a hissing tone. "How dare you dupe me this way, you bastard?"

"That wasn't my intention," Cal said, his tone matching his features.

Emma laughed without humor. "Oh, please, don't insult my intelligence."

Patrick circled her shoulders with his arm and pulled her and Logan close to his side. "You're wasting your time talking to this s.o.b. You don't owe him anything."

The charged atmosphere heightened.

"You're right, she doesn't," Cal replied.

Emma continued to stare at Cal with loathing. "You had to know you'd get caught." In spite of her efforts to hold her voice steady, she couldn't. Her entire body was trembling so much she was amazed her legs continued to support her.

"I had every intention of telling you myself," Cal said, his harsh voice scraping over her raw nerves.

A shrill laughter erupted, then Emma said in a voice that bore no resemblance to her own because of the fury that was almost choking her. "Yeah, right."

"Get the hell out of our sight," Patrick spat. "Now."

Cal's eyes delved into hers; his jaw was rigid. "Is that what you want, Emma?"

Another bout of fury rose up that threatened to consume her. She wanted to attack, to scratch his eyes out for making a fool of her. She did neither. She held her ground and said in a frigid tone, "I not only want you out of my sight now, I don't ever want to see you again."

"I'm afraid that's not going to happen."

Emma felt her cheeks blister as fear charged through her with the force of a major tornado. Her worst nightmare was about to come to fruition. But not if she could help it, she thought savagely, jerking herself up by the bootstraps.

She'd never been a weakling when it came to a good fight, and she wasn't about to turn into one now, not when there was so much at stake. She would dig deeper for the strength and courage to win this battle.

But win she would.

Only he's not my son. Not yet.

Her knees almost buckled when that dose of reality struck her like a sledgehammer.

Logan's whimpering suddenly claimed her attention. "It's all right, darling. Mommy's here."

"Where's that damn doctor?" Cal muttered.

"You're not staying," Emma responded in a tight voice. "You have no right."

Cal stepped forward, a gleam of anger in his eyes. "You know better than that."

Emma felt her chin wobble, and though she hated for him to see her fear, she couldn't help it. Her baby's face was bleeding along with her heart. "No, I don't," she finally responded. "You don't know for sure Logan's *your* son."

"As long as my name's on the birth certificate, which we both know is the case, he's mine."

"Go away, Cal." Emma's voice was as dull as the ache building inside her.

"I'll go as soon as my son is taken care of."

Suddenly Emma heard her name called by the receptionist. Clinging to Logan as her lifeline, she swung around and headed for the door that was now open. It was only after she was seated in a cubicle that she realized she wasn't alone. She bristled.

"I told you I'm not leaving," Cal said in a terse voice.

Though Emma had to grit her teeth to keep from starting another verbal slinging match, she did just that. Besides, she no longer had the energy. She felt drained to the max, and if that tight rein she had on her emotions slipped one iota, she would crack like a hollow nut.

Anyway, there wasn't time. A tall, young doctor came through the door and said, "What have we here?"

With relief washing through her, Emma turned her back on Cal, who was using the wall to prop himself up, and concentrated on the doctor and his examination of Logan.

Twenty minutes later she had an exhausted baby in her arms and was on her way out of the E.R. Patrick's protective arm was around her while tears of relief streamed from her eyes. Logan's injury was not serious. No stitches had been required; a butterfly bandage had been the course of action.

"Just watch him closely for the rest of the day and night," Dr. Jacobs had said.

"What should I watch for?" Emma had asked, feeling her fear mount again.

"If he gets sick to his tummy or breaks out with perspiration, call me. That could indicate a slight concussion."

"But you don't think that will happen." Emma didn't bother to temper the frantic note in her voice.

"No. Otherwise, I'd keep him for observation overnight. But I'd be negligent in my duty if I didn't alert you to that possibility."

With that thought uppermost in her mind, Emma realized she wouldn't close her eyes during the night, which she also realized wasn't in her best interest. She knew she would ruminate about Cal and how he'd betrayed her.

Damn him.

"Watch your step, honey," Patrick said.

Startled out of her daze, Emma saw they had reached her dad's truck. She also saw that Cal had followed. Furious at his continued intrusion, she swung around and lashed out, "One more time, stay away from us."

"No can do." His drawling voice had a harsh edge to it.

"You have no choice," Emma said fiercely. "He's mine."

Cal's features were twisted. "Until the court decides otherwise."

"You bastard."

"I'll concede that."

"So you do have a conscience," she said, hope suddenly springing inside her.

"I'm sorry I deceived you, but I can't give up my son." Cal paused and narrowed his eyes. "And that's nonnegotiable."

Having said that, he whipped around and made his way to his truck, brutally crushing any hope that she'd seen the last of him. She didn't move until he'd left the parking lot.

"Get in," Patrick said. After he'd pulled out of the lot himself, Emma felt his eyes on her. "Don't you worry for one minute. That bastard won't get near you and Logan again."

"What…" She struggled to speak. "What if I…don't have a choice?" Emma whispered around the lump knotted in her throat.

"Oh, we'll have a choice, all right," Patrick said with bitterness. "My attorney will see to that."

Emma didn't respond. Instead, she bent her head, kissed Logan's exposed cheek, the trace of tears still visible, and held him ever so tightly.

"It's going to be a fight, I'm here to tell you that."

Though Emma knew that fact deep down, she didn't want to hear it verbalized by her dad's attorney. Also deep down she didn't want the facts sugarcoated, either.

"Dammit, Russ, whose side are you on, anyway?"

Emma heard the hostility in Patrick's voice and watched to see what effect it would have on Russ Hinson, who was supposed to be a crackerjack lawyer in the practice of family law.

"You know whose side I'm on," Russ shot back, rising to his feet, which exposed a girth around his middle that indicated he'd rather eat than exercise.

"Are you telling us we can't stop Cal?" Emma asked before her father could speak again.

"Thank you, Emma, for seeing the light." Russ didn't bother to hide a trace of sarcasm.

"Why the hell can't we?" Patrick demanded, as though determined to have the last word. "That's what I'm offering to pay you big bucks for."

"Money can't buy everything, Dad," Emma said, sick at heart at the turn of events.

"The hell it can't."

When Patrick had told her he wanted to go see his attorney, she'd told him that was all right, as long as the visit was short. She wanted Logan in familiar circumstances. Now, she almost wished she'd told her dad to take her home instead.

"Emma's right," Russ said. "I'm here to tell you money's not always the cure-all, and you know that, Patrick. At this moment, you're grasping for straws. I understand that."

"So are you telling us there's nothing we can do?" Fear dried out her throat. "That we have no options, that this...this man will be able to take my child?"

"He's not your child, Emma. You only have guardianship, and it's temporary, at that."

Though Russ's voice was gentle, his reminder jabbed at her heart again, leaving her feeling perilously close to tears. "Would a permanent guardianship have made a difference?"

"Probably not."

Despair threatened to overwhelm her. "So what do we do, Russ?"

"We fight."

"But you just said we didn't—" Emma broke off with a stammer, staring at him wide-eyed, clearly conflicted about what she was hearing.

"Look, you two, while Cal has a chance to get Logan eventually, that's not going to happen any time soon."

"You know that for sure?" Emma asked and wasn't sorry even after Russ looked at her with disdain.

"You have to trust me, Emma, and you, too, Patrick, to do what I think will be in your best interest. Certainly Logan's."

"I do, but—" Again Emma's voice failed.

"The first order is to make sure Webster is the biological father through DNA testing." Russ paused and rubbed his girth. "If not, then this brouhaha's dead in the water before it ever gets off the ground."

"That's true," Emma said, feeling the knot in her tummy ease a bit.

"So how are you going to handle Webster?" Patrick asked, the bitterness still very much in his tone. "I want that s.o.b. nailed to the wall."

"I thought this was about Logan, about getting custody of him," the attorney said.

Emma watched the color drain from Patrick's face. He didn't like his hand being called on anything. He was used to people catering to him because of his money and prestige. And while his behavior oftentimes made his daughter uncomfortable, today was not one of those times. If his assets could make Logan hers, then so be it.

"It is, dammit," Patrick said, hostility once again filtering through his tone.

"Dad, please, just let Russ handle it, okay?"

He turned and faced her. "All right, Emma, we'll try it your way."

She turned back to Russ. "I need to get Logan home. Call me and let me know what I'm supposed to do."

"You'll be the first to know. Until then, don't worry. It's going to be okay."

Now, as Emma curled up on the sofa, a glass of warm milk in hand, she couldn't seem to stop thinking about that conversation that had taken place in Russ's office immediately after they'd left the hospital.

Even though it was bedtime, she'd known sleep would be impossible. She'd been right. It was half past midnight and here she was sitting in the living room, her eyes wired open.

Fear.

Of Cal Webster.

That was what had her in its clutches and wouldn't let go.

Again, she couldn't believe she'd been so gullible, *such a patsy,* in falling for his charm and not recognizing that she was being duped by a wolf in sheep's clothing. And to think she'd wanted to make love to him. Suddenly her insides felt ice-cold. But in defense of herself, how could she have known?

While she couldn't answer that question, Emma held herself fully accountable. And though she was loath to admit it, she still found him attractive. Even at the hospital, she'd been aware of his presence with every nerve in her body.

She had even felt a pang when she'd seen a flash of vulnerability in his otherwise tough facade.

"Stop it," she muttered. This was no time to feel anything for him but contempt and anger. Since she'd learned his true identity and his full betrayal, he had become the enemy.

Yet she couldn't halt the track of her mind, which kept going back to the way he'd made her feel, how she'd craved more of those hot, deep kisses. When he'd touched her breasts—it had been like heaven—she'd wondered how it would feel to have him inside, riding until they both climaxed in unison.

A mortified cry escaped Emma's lips.

How could she think thoughts like that, especially when she knew he was out to take her child? Was she cut from the same bolt of cloth as her sister after all?

Suddenly her brain seemed to boil. Her sister. How could it even cross her mind to have sex with her sister's ex-husband? The thought should be repulsive and disgusting. In order to stave off the pain ravaging her, Emma folded her arms across her stomach and rocked back and forth.

How long she remained in that rocking position, she didn't know. What she did know was that she wasn't about to give up or in. If it was a fight Cal Webster wanted, then by damn, a fight he would get.

"I won't give up my baby," Emma sobbed, "I won't."

Twelve

Cal felt awful.

He hated that feeling; in fact, it agitated him no end. But what the hell? He'd been thrown a curveball he hadn't expected, although he should have, he reminded himself with a mental kick in the rear.

His horse snorted, making Cal aware that he had stopped in the middle of the pasture, facing the east where the sun was making its presence known in the most incredible way. Even though his mare appeared impatient and slightly skittish, having recently been broken, Cal wasn't.

What a beautiful sight, he thought. His eyes leveled on the sky in the distance. A deep sigh escaped him. He'd missed this while he'd been undercover. Because of that he couldn't seem to get enough of the wide-open spaces for more reasons than one. He could do his best thinking with nature surrounding him.

However, *thinking* was not what he needed to do.

Nothing had worked out the way he'd hoped, guilt continuing to fill every crevice of his being. Finally nudging the mare into movement, he guided her to a tree and dismounted. He grabbed his thermos out of his pack and poured himself a full cup of coffee. His intention was to finish repairing the broken fence. Again, Art had offered to help and again Cal had told him no, that he'd do it. He wanted the exercise in hopes of getting his mind off what he was facing.

Somehow he suspected that wasn't going to happen, no matter how hard he worked his body. Another sigh filtered through his lips at the same time he shoved his hat back on his head. Along with the sun, the humidity was rising, meaning he'd sweat like a pig when he began this chore.

Suddenly, mending that fence didn't hold the charm it once had. Maybe he ought to let Art do it, after all. He thought on that for a moment, then muttered, "Nah." He then trudged to his pack for hammer and staples.

A couple of hours later he was back under the huge oak, his breath coming in gulps while his heart beat like crazy, making him feel slightly dizzy. It took two bottles of Gatorade before he felt like himself again.

Or close to it.

He knew better than to try and make his body a whipping post. That tactic failed every time. He ought to know; he'd tried it in the past. He'd have to find another kinder, gentler way to deal with his thoughts of Emma and Logan.

No matter how much he tried they wouldn't disappear from his mind or his heart. It was as though they had been imprinted permanently in both places.

"Damn," Cal muttered, removing his hat and wiping the sweat from his forehead.

Why did he feel like the bad guy in this whole affair?

So he'd lied to her, even though at the time it had been unintentional. Still, he had lied, which he regretted now, of course. But it was too late. He could suck on those sour grapes forever, and it wouldn't change what he'd done. He guessed what really had him in an uproar was that his attorney had managed to get the case on the court docket for the day after tomorrow.

He had no choice but to forge ahead with his plans to get visitation rights. At a later date, a custody hearing was sure to follow—unless he and Emma could work something out in the meantime.

That wasn't going to happen. Why? While he definitely wanted his son, he wanted Emma as well. He didn't want one without the other. Admitting that to himself was such a shock it gave Cal the weak trembles. In fact, he couldn't believe he'd let himself travel down that path, knowing it had no good end.

He'd seen nothing but loathing in Emma's eyes in the E.R., and he knew her feelings hadn't changed. Since they had become involved, he had so hoped he could bypass this court appearance and reach an amicable agreement concerning visitation.

No chance of that now.

By not being up-front with her, he'd cooked his own goose. She'd never trust him again. He groaned inwardly. He couldn't blame her either. If the shoe had been on the other foot, he'd feel the same way.

No one liked being made a fool of, and that was exactly what he'd done to her. Suddenly Cal felt a bout of queasiness hit him, which only added to his frustration.

If only he didn't have feelings for Emma, how much easier it would be to fight for his child. If only...if only. He could play that unproductive game forever, too, and it wouldn't accomplish anything.

Except to make him feel more guilty.

He let an expletive rip, then pulled his foot off the tree and headed back to the nearly finished fence. An hour later found Cal back at the cabin, showered and dressed.

It was when he reached for his cell phone that he spotted the blinking red signal. After he saw who the caller was, his former boss, his brows met in a troubled frown. He'd deal with him later.

He'd hoped against hope that it might be Emma. "That's not in the cards, Webster," he said aloud. "You made sure of that."

After Cal had left the hospital, feeling dead inside, he'd gone to Hammond and told him to get the proceedings in the works ASAP. Luckily, the attorney had been able to do just that.

Cal's thinking at that point had been to get this matter settled without delay, in light of the mental whipping he'd taken from Emma and her father. If Patrick hadn't been in the mix, perhaps things would be different. But since the old man was involved, it would be a fight to the finish.

Cal hadn't liked Patrick before or after he'd married Connie. He liked him even less now. Patrick took himself far too seriously.

How in heaven's name had he managed to get involved with two women from the same family? The fact that they were sisters was even more mind-boggling.

Though he needed his head examined for getting

himself into this predicament, he was in it and had no choice but to see it through, no matter what the outcome.

But when it came to Connie and Emma, there was no comparison. Lust, instead of love, had been the tie that bound him to his ex, lust that had quickly faded. While he certainly didn't love Emma, he felt much more than lust for her, though that was certainly part of his feelings. He also felt a tenderness, a need to protect her, to shield her from pain and heartache.

Right now, just thinking about those luscious lips and voluptuous breasts, both of which he'd felt, started a bonfire in his groin that threatened to consume him. He longed to kiss and lick every succulent part of her body.

That out-of-control fire in his lower extremity was what caused him to do something that had heretofore been out of the question.

He punched in Emma's number, feeling his heartbeat in the back of his throat. He had no idea what he was going to say to her should she answer.

"What do you want?"

The shock of hearing her voice robbed him of speech for a second, but then he rallied. Although the hostility was obvious, he wasn't about to renege on his courage now. He'd bitten the bullet and wasn't going to spit it out—not before he'd had his say, that is.

As a result, he said the first thing that came to mind. In retrospect, not a smart move. Nonetheless, he couldn't take the words back. "I want to see you."

"Well, I don't want to see you."

Cal rubbed the back of his neck, but it didn't help unkink the muscles. They just kinked that much tighter, along with the rest of his body. Dammit, he had to get hold of himself.

"Look, Emma, if I told you I was sorry, would it make a difference?"

"What do you think?"

"No."

"Need I say more," she said in that same low, hostile tone.

Cal's lips flatlined while he tried to regroup, hoping to try another tactic that might restore some civility between them. The way things were, communication was almost impossible.

"Please, don't ever call me again," she said in a faltering voice.

"Emma, we have to talk. We have no choice."

"You're wrong about that, Cal."

He flinched at the way she said his name, like she'd tasted something foreign and bitter. This was much harder than he'd thought. But then, he hadn't *thought*. That was the problem.

"We all have choices," she pointed out. "You've made yours and I've made mine."

"That's unacceptable to me."

"I'm sorry."

"I didn't mean to hurt you, Emma."

"You lied to me, Cal. You betrayed me."

"I know, and I'm sorry."

"Why did you do it?"

"Would you believe me if I told you I don't know?"

"No, I wouldn't."

He released a pent-up sigh. "I don't want to fight you over Logan, especially not in court."

"I don't want that, either."

"Then let's talk."

"I can't," she said in a low, unsteady voice. "You want to take my baby away from me."

"Right now I only want the right to see my son."

Silence.

"Couldn't we just bypass the courts and work that out between us?"

Another silence.

"Emma, please."

"I'm sorry, Cal, I don't think that's in Logan's best interest."

He barely contained his temper. But to lose it now wouldn't serve any purpose except to make matters worse. God, they were bad enough as it was.

"I hope you know what you're doing, Emma."

"That works both ways."

With that tumultuous reply, she hung up, leaving him staring at the dark, dead screen on his cell. Fighting a bout of temper and frustration, he slammed it shut and pinched the bridge of his nose with his fingers.

So much for trying to settle out of court, he thought with a pang of regret. The idea of seeing Emma again under such adverse circumstances tore at his gut. But what option did he have? None, unless a miracle happened between now and the appointed time. After what his job had put him through, he no longer believed in miracles.

Another expletive shot out of Cal's mouth in conjunction with a knock on the door. Pulling a face, he stomped to the front and jerked the door open.

"Hello, Webster."

Every muscle in his body tensed. "What are you doing here?"

"Is that any way to greet your boss?"

"Ex, might I remind you."

Tony Richards shrugged with a brief smile. "Something tells me you're not happy to see me."

Cal didn't bother to answer.

"Aren't you going to invite me in?"

"I don't see any reason for that," Cal said with conviction.

He meant what he'd said, too. The last person he needed intruding in his life right now was this man. Tony didn't care about anything, or anyone, except the bureau. He was their best by-the-books man. Cal was certain that was how Tony got off, by giving his entire loyalty to the agency.

Thus, they were as far apart on the spectrum as they could possibly be.

"I know why the bureau got rid of you, Webster. You're an ass."

"They didn't get rid of me. I got rid of them."

Tony shrugged. "Whatever."

"Find someone else to finish the job," Cal said, getting down to the nitty-gritty.

"No can do," Tony said. "It's your case. You're the only one who can tie up the loose ends."

"And if I refuse?"

Tony's thin features twisted. "We both know you're not going to do that."

"Dammit, Tony, I don't need this right now."

"That's your problem, not mine." Having said that, he swept by Cal and didn't stop until he'd reached the middle of the living room. He turned then and said; "Sit down, we have to talk."

Fighting off a feeling of dread, Cal slammed the door

and made his way to the fireplace where he leaned against it, folded his arms across his chest and glared at his cohort. "I'm listening," he said in a hard, cold voice.

Thirteen

Emma had cried until she couldn't cry anymore.

Only, her sobs had changed nothing. The court date had come and gone and she had lost. Cal had gained visitation rights to his son, and she had no alternative but to comply.

The judge, whom her father considered a close friend, had let them down. Without much thought, or so it seemed to her, the decision had been made. Cut and dried. No discussion. Cal had won and that was that.

Emma suspected the fact that her attorney called Cal's and insisted on him having a DNA test had probably played a huge part in the judge's decision. The test had proven that Cal was indeed Logan's biological father.

Even so, her father had been livid, feeling as though *he'd* been betrayed by a lifetime friend.

As a result, Emma had had to stop him from stomping into the judge's chambers afterwards and confronting him.

"Dad." She'd grabbed hold of his arm, digging her fingers into it. "Don't even think about it."

"Dammit, he's my friend. How could he do this to you...to us?"

"I don't know," she whispered. It was hard to comfort him when her own heart was breaking. But she had enough of her faculties left to know Judge Rivers wouldn't think twice about slapping Patrick in jail if he attacked verbally or physically.

She couldn't have stood that. Her daddy was all she had to lean on; nothing could happen to him, not out of stupidity, anyway.

As if he sensed what was going through her mind, Patrick had halted his steps. "I have to do something," he said fiercely. "Maybe I'll just have a set-to with Webster."

"No, Daddy, no," she said in a terse tone. "That will also get you in trouble. Stay away from him, too."

Though Patrick had listened, she knew it stuck in his craw. She suspected he would do what he wanted when she wasn't around.

As for herself, she hadn't looked at Cal at any time throughout the ordeal. It was only after the verdict had been rendered that their gazes had accidentally connected and held.

Just thinking about those few seconds filled Emma with added shame. Instead of staring at him like he wasn't even there, like he was a nonentity, she'd actually been aware of everything about him, from what he had on—a crisp white shirt, jeans and boots—to the way he'd stood rigid and unbending, to the heavy-lidded look in his eyes that had a sensuality that took her breath.

There was another emotion that was even more disturbing. She had seen a flash of pain in those blue wells, some-thing she hadn't wanted to see or acknowledge.

Rather, she'd wanted to feel nothing for him except hatred and contempt.

Jerking her thoughts away from that awful moment three days ago did little to calm her now. Emma's body suddenly felt bathed in sweat, her skin cold and clammy. How was she going to stand the pain? How was she going to endure seeing Cal every time he came for Logan?

Though the answer was inconceivable to her, she knew she'd do what she'd always done when a crisis threatened to rip her life apart—she'd simply dig deeper for strength and courage and muddle through.

But, dear God, this was her child. *Not yet,* that little voice whispered. *Maybe never,* that same little voice taunted. She pressed her hands over her ears, praying that her emotions would become numb, that she would cease to feel.

That didn't happen. Her stomach churned. For a second Emma thought she might actually lose its contents. She didn't see how that could be possible since she didn't have anything there to begin with.

She'd skipped breakfast and lunch. With dinnertime fast approaching, she felt no desire to eat now either. She'd worked harder today than she had in weeks, desperate to keep her mind occupied so she wouldn't keep dwelling on the horrifying thoughts that constantly nipped at her heels.

She couldn't lose her child. She saw visitation rights as the first step toward that. If Cal were to eventually win custody, he could take Logan out of the country.

She'd want to die.

Emma blew out a trembling breath, but it didn't help untie the knot of fear in her stomach. Since they had left the courthouse, she had expected Cal, knowing that it was only a matter of time until he showed up for his first visit.

To think he had permission to see Logan alone made her even crazier. If Cal tried that, Logan would not be receptive. The child would cry his little heart out. It was thinking of Logan's tears that made Emma realize that *she* was crying. *Again.*

Maybe Cal would change his mind. Maybe he would decide none of this was good for the child. Of course that wasn't about to happen. In her heart of hearts, she knew that. Yet thinking it helped maintain her sanity.

Cal felt he had the right to share in his son's life. Maybe he did. But again, to think there was even the remotest possibility that Cal would whisk him away at a future date to some foreign country was inconceivable. It just couldn't happen.

Only, it could.

There were countless stories in the news and on television that bore testimony to that. Women lost a child to that kind of evil every day. But please, God, not her, she begged, raising her head to the ceiling.

It was then that the phone rang. Emma almost didn't answer, but when she saw who was calling, she reached for the receiver, her heart in her throat.

"Hello, Russ," she said, her breathing shallow. Attorneys rarely called with good news.

"I have a date on the custody hearing."

Her breathing faltered yet again. "Already?"

"Yes. According to his attorney, Webster's on a short leash time-wise."

"Well, that's just too bad," she said with all the bitterness she could muster.

Russ's sigh filtered through the line. "I know how you feel, my dear. But don't throw in the towel just yet."

"That's the last thing I'm going to do, Russ. You know that. I'm going to fight to the bitter end and longer. I'll do whatever it takes to keep my baby."

"You're preaching to the choir. I'm on your side, remember?"

"Then why is Cal allowed to see my son?" She knew she was babbling without cause. Russ had argued with a fierceness that had surprised even her, being the mild-mannered man he was. But it hadn't done any good.

"Emma—"

She heard the frustration in his voice and knew she'd stepped on a nerve. "Sorry, Russ. That was a cheap shot and I'm sorry."

"Not a problem. I know how frightened and frustrated you are. After all, I have children of my own. But hold on to the fact that visitation rights are a whole different ball game from his getting full custody. Judge Rivers is not about to rip Logan out of your arms, not at this point, anyway."

But there was a point at which that could happen. That was what continued to drive her insane. "Thanks, Russ," was all she was capable of saying.

"Make a note of the date."

With trembling fingers, she did just that.

"By the way, has Webster seen Logan yet?"

"No."

"Mmm, that surprises me."

"Me, too. Every time I walk out the door or anywhere else, I look over my shoulder, expecting to see him."

"When you least expect him, that's when he'll show."

"That's what I'm afraid of."

"Keep your chin up, sweetheart. As I said earlier, it ain't over till it's over."

"In other words, the fat lady hasn't sung yet?" Hope sprang eternal.

"That's right. Keep that attitude and you'll come out the winner."

Once she'd replaced the receiver, Emma's stomach churned again. As a precaution, she scurried into her bathroom, only to pull up short, her hand flying to her chest.

"Damn," she said, watching as water poured from under the commode, then eventually around her feet.

She grabbed a towel, fell to her knees, and began mopping up the water, tears of frustration falling from her eyes.

"Move over. I'll do that."

She froze. Literally.

Cal?

No way. Surely the fact that she was an emotional wreck had brought on this hallucination.

"Emma."

Oh, Lord , it *was* Cal, speaking to her in that low, raspy voice that now held an edge of harshness.

Fear lumped in her stomach, keeping her from responding. Then she felt strong hands close around her bare arms and lift her. Don't touch me, she wanted to scream. But nothing came out of her mouth. She was only conscious of goose bumps lining her spine because he was *touching* her.

How could she react to him in a sexual way when he'd so blatantly broken her heart? Because she had missed him, her heart whispered. But how could that be when he was clearly the enemy? Even though shame and disgust ran through her, Emma couldn't seem to control them.

"Please, let me go," she said when she was finally on her feet, facing him, only then to find the sight of him captured her breath.

"Now that you're upright, that's not a problem.

"Careful," he cautioned when she appeared to teeter.

"I'm...fine."

He dropped his arms and simply stared at her.

Stepping back out of harm's way, she licked her lips, trying to relieve some of the dryness that kept her from speaking. Later, she convinced herself that it was her imagination, but she thought she heard him utter a muted groan as his gaze locked on her lips.

"This is no job for a woman." His voice was gritty.

"I can do it."

"I'm sure you can, only you're not going to."

She wanted to argue, but she didn't have the strength. Seeing him had drained her. Right now, watching him drop to his knees and reach for the water cutoff valve, she found herself mesmerized by the sight of his tight ass before her eyes and face, envisioning that part of his anatomy naked with her cupping both of those cheeks in her hands.

Biting down on her lower lip was the only thing that saved her from crying out. Shame such as she'd never felt before rocked her.

"I need to see about Logan." Without waiting for an answer, Emma fled to the baby's room and latched onto the railing of the play pen with both hands, squeezing it for all she was worth.

She didn't know how long she stood there before Cal

appeared in the doorway, a shuttered expression on his face. "I think I've got it fixed. The floor is cleaned up as well."

"Thank you," she forced herself to say, conscious of him with every fiber of her being.

"You're welcome."

Silence.

"Look, I'm sorry I just barged in."

"Then why did you?"

"I knocked." He shrugged. "When you didn't answer, I tried the door and it was unlocked."

"I never leave my front door unlocked," she said more to herself than him.

"I'm glad, since that's not a good idea."

Another silence.

"What are you doing here?" she asked, breaking the uneasy silence that had fallen.

"You know the answer to that."

She bowed her head. "I wish you had called first."

"I thought it might be easier just to show up."

"Easier for whom?"

"Look, Emma, I don't want to start World War Three."

"What *do* you want?" A stupid question, she told herself. One she shouldn't have asked.

Cal swerved his gaze. "For now, to see my son."

After a shaken silence, she said, "He's sleeping."

This time his gaze speared her. "I'll just wait until he wakes up."

"What if that's unacceptable?"

Once again she was impaled by the unnerving intensity of his gaze. "I'll wait anyway."

Fourteen

Emma felt cold suddenly, so cold that it was all she could do to keep her teeth from banging together.

"Look, the last thing I want is to cause you more pain."

She heard the anguish and the frustration in Cal's tone, but she couldn't let that get to her. She had to remain strong and unyielding in her efforts to keep her emotions intact.

"I can read your mind, Emma. I know you think I'm the big, bad wolf who's come to whisk Logan away from you forever."

"Aren't you?" she asked around the growing lump in her throat.

He regarded her with intense, unreadable eyes before saying, "No. That's not my intention at all."

Emma gnawed on her lower lip to keep it from trembling. God, this was so hard because she felt so inept, so out of control.

"But I can't just walk away." He paused. "If the shoe were on the other foot, you couldn't either."

"So I guess we're at an impasse," she said with passionate belligerence.

"We can work through this." Cal shoved a hand through his hair. "I know we can. But I just don't have the answer."

"I do," she said without hesitation. "Just walk away."

"And let you have him?"

She didn't respond, but he knew her answer.

He cursed. "You're the most stubborn woman I've ever come in contact with."

"If you cared about Logan, you wouldn't do this." Emma was desperately trying to appeal to his soft side, his conscience, *anything,* that would get his attention. "I meant what I said. Walk away and leave us alone."

"You're not just talking about for now, are you? About visitation rights?"

The room was suddenly warm, too warm. "No," she said in a strangled voice. "I'm talking about forever."

"That's not going to happen."

The light had gone out of his eyes, reminding her of empty holes. Still, they held steady.

"I'm not leaving until I see my boy." His tone sounded set in stone.

Emma feared that would be the case, that once he got his foot in the door, such as now, he wouldn't ever turn and walk away. Who in their right mind could leave Logan, such a precious loving child?

"I know I can't stop you, but—" Emma's voice faded as the reality of the situation finally dawned on her. She had no choice in the matter. The court had ruled in his

favor, and she couldn't refuse him access to his child.
Now. Tomorrow. Or the next day.

Her soul was weeping, and though Emma wanted to
conceal that fact from him, fearing he would use that vulnerability as a weapon against her, she wasn't sure she could.

"There are no buts, Emma," he said in a gentle tone.

Don't be nice to me, she almost shouted. She wanted
to hate him for the pain he'd caused her, for the pain he
was *causing* her.

"I'll try and stay out of your way. I promise."

"And just how do you propose to do that?" she asked
with contempt.

"Wait in the living room, I suppose." His tone was now
weary.

Before she could answer, she heard Logan cry. She
skirted around Cal and made her way to the child, ever
conscious of Cal. Logan now stood in the play pen, his
arms outstretched. "Mama," he cried, though his eyes went
beyond her shoulder.

"How are you, kiddo?" Cal asked, grinning.

Logan answered with a grin of his own, then began
bouncing up and down. "Mind if I take him?" Cal instantly raised a hand. "Forget I asked that. Of course, you
mind," he said with bitterness.

"He won't go to you." Emma's tone was smug.

Cal merely lifted his eyebrows before extending his arms
and reaching for the baby. "Man, what a big boy you are."

Emma looked on, expecting any moment to hear
Logan tune up and cry, especially after he realized a
stranger had him. Much to her shock and chagrin that
never happened.

Logan seemed completely content to have Cal hold

him. In fact, he reached out, grabbed Cal's nose and began pulling on it, a silly grin crinkling his little face.

"I need to change his diaper," Emma said, an undisguised sharpness in her tone.

"Can't it wait a minute?"

"No," Emma said in a waspish tone, letting her jealousy show. She couldn't help it. She could hardly bear the thought of Cal holding Logan, much less bonding with him. That was a blow she wasn't prepared for, nor could she accept.

"You wanna see what I brought you?" Cal asked Logan, after she had changed his diaper.

Silently, they made their way into the living room where Cal set Logan on the floor, and, holding him with one hand, he reached for a package on the sofa.

"I didn't know you had brought him something," Emma said in that same waspish tone.

Cal looked at her, and for a split second, their eyes held. No, please, she cried silently, especially after her heart went into overdrive. She didn't want to feel anything for this man ever again except hatred.

"I didn't have a chance to say anything," he said in a warm voice, "not after I found you on the bathroom floor mopping up water, that is."

Emma's face scrunched up, then she said in a stilted tone, "I haven't properly thanked you for that."

A grin played with Cal's lips. "Don't. It was my pleasure."

She looked down before he could read her mind and see the conflicting emotions that raged inside her.

"Okay, buddy, why don't you see what's inside this sack?" Cal sat on the floor beside Logan and let the child mangle the paper.

With a resigned sigh, Emma sat on the sofa and watched father and son together, praying that she wouldn't see any resemblance between them.

No such luck.

With their heads almost touching, while Cal explained what the fire engine was all about, Emma noticed Logan had Cal's nose and chin. More obvious were the eyes. Logan had those same blue pools set deep in his head.

Why had she never picked up on something so obvious?

Because she hadn't been looking for it. Now that she'd been blindsided with the unvarnished truth, it was so clear. And so *frightening,* realizing again that she could lose her baby.

While it was extremely difficult to watch the continued interplay between them, she couldn't remove her gaze either, seeing a side of Cal she hadn't known existed. But then there was a lot about him she didn't pretend to know.

If only she could hate him, how much easier things would be. Only she did hate him, she told herself quickly. *Liar.* She didn't hate him at all and therein lay the problem. Despite the havoc and devastation he had wreaked in her life, she still cared about him, still wanted him to touch her, to kiss her, *to make love to her.*

She must have made a sound because Cal's head came up and around, his gaze trapping hers. Heat flared between them while her eyes dipped to the mound behind his zipper before another dose of reality struck her.

Dragging her eyes away from what lay between his legs, she once again waged a battle with her humiliation and shame.

At a time like this, how could she think such a thing?

"Emma, we have to talk," Cal said, breaking into her torturous thoughts with a sultry edge to his voice.

She hardened her heart. "There's nothing left to say."

"That's not true and you know it. I saw the way you looked at me."

Appalled, she sucked in her breath and held it.

"Sorry, I shouldn't have said that."

"Why not?" she asked bitterly. "It's the truth."

A muscle twitched in his jaw, and his eyes gleamed with renewed fire. When he spoke, he seemed to ignore the heightened sexual tension that enveloped the room. "Logan's a great kid. I have you to thank for that."

"He's a baby, not a kid."

Cal's lips tightened, but again his tone was nonconfrontational. "You're not going to drive me away, Emma."

She gritted her teeth. "I know that."

"Good." He returned his attention to Logan who was beginning to fuss, apparently from the loss of attention, having grown tired of the truck.

"There's something else in the sack." Cal tore it open wider, then took Logan's hand and placed it inside. Seconds later, the baby drew out a rubber toy which went immediately to his mouth. Only not for long. He then handed the toy to Cal who took it and pretended to gnaw on it, making chomping noises.

In spite of her efforts to the contrary, Emma felt her eyes mist as Logan giggled in a shrill voice. Though every part of her soul ached at the interchange, she did acknowledge that Cal had a way with his child.

No matter, she reaffirmed stubbornly. She still wasn't about to give him up without a fight. And while she had to pull in her claws for the moment, it didn't mean she would forever. She'd comply with the court order, and get along, saving her big guns for the custody battle that was yet to come.

The way Emma saw it, World War Three couldn't be avoided.

Logan's whimper refocused her attention. He was toddling toward her, his arms outstretched. "Mama."

"I'm here, precious," she said, scooping him up and sitting him on her lap.

Feeling Cal's eyes on her, Emma lowered her head and snuggled Logan's neck, ignoring Cal's efforts to regain her attention.

His harsh sigh brought her head back up only to see he'd gotten to his feet. "Thanks for the time."

"Are you going?" she asked with surprise.

A mocking smile lightened his features. "Are you asking me to stay?"

"No," she snapped.

"Didn't think so."

A silence ensued.

Cal spoke at last. "I'd like to take him to the ranch."

"When?" Emma demanded, aghast.

"Tomorrow."

"I don't—"

"I'm supposed to see him twice this week, and tomorrow's Saturday."

"I...we have other plans."

The furrow between Cal's brow deepened. "Cancel them."

She gasped. "You can't order me around."

"I want you to come, too." His tone was bleak. "Please."

That last word came out as a plea, which ignited a

flame in the pit of her stomach. She then stared into his tormented face and stammered, "All right, we'll go."

Emma hated to admit it, but she was having a good time. More importantly, Logan was really enjoying himself. She had made sure she'd coated his face, arms and legs with sunscreen, knowing they would be outdoors the majority of the time.

She'd been right.

When they had arrived at the ranch a couple of hours ago, Cal had stopped by the house and grabbed an old-fashioned picnic basket and a cooler. A short time later found them in a perfect meadow close to where his horses were penned.

For the longest time, they both followed Logan, who had been in awe of everything, from Cal's yard dog Charlie, to the ducks on the nearby pond, to the butterflies flickering about, hankering to touch them all.

Finally, Logan had run down, and Emma put him down on the pallet for a nap. That was a good thing for Logan, but not for her. With him non-mobile, it left her alone with Cal.

She was far too conscious of him and his every move. Even now, she could smell the distinctive scent of his cologne, which was terribly disturbing and distracting.

In fact, she only had to move a hair's breadth and she could rub her leg against his. She fought against that forbidden urge. She didn't want to feel that sudden rush of excitement when they were together like this, when their eyes met or their hands accidentally touched. Instead, she wanted to remain aloof, angry and unresponsive.

Only that wasn't happening. He was just too much of a sexy animal; his nearness threatened to overwhelm her.

"Have you had a good time?"

Cal's question brought her head around. "Yes, I have," she admitted with reluctance.

He smiled. "I'm glad."

That smile was her undoing. Tears welled in her eyes, and she turned away, but apparently not before he'd seen the liquid trickling down her face.

"Hey," he said in a husky voice, "don't do that."

"I don't want to," she muttered fiercely. "It's just that—" She clamped her mouth shut in order not to start another argument. Besides, it wouldn't do her any good. For now, Cal's presence was simply a bitter pill she had to swallow.

"You're ripping my guts to pieces," Cal said. "But you know that."

His gravelly voice scraped across Emma's frayed nerves, leaving her feeling more vulnerable than ever. "Please. Let's not go there."

He took a shaky breath. "You can't deny what's between us, Emma."

"Yes, I can," she said through tight lips.

His gaze locked on her with laser-like intensity. However, before he could say anything, Art came through the trees and called, "Hey, y'all."

Startled, they both whipped around. In doing so they awakened Logan.

"Mama," he cried, reaching for her.

"It's okay, sweetie. Mommy's here."

"Duck." Logan pointed at the pond.

Art reached the pallet and tipped his hat to Emma, winked at Logan, then faced Cal. "I penned the stallion and saddled him just in case you might want to work with him later. As you know, he needs to get more used to being saddled."

"Much obliged," Cal drawled. "I might just do that."

Emma frowned as her eyes wandered toward the corral. "He looks big and scary."

Cal smiled down at her, sending tingles through her. "Nah. Looks can be deceiving. I've been slowly but surely breaking him in. But I'm not training him while you and Logan are here." He paused. "Unless you'd like to see how I…we work together."

"It's fine with me."

"I'll take care of the boy, Ms. Jenkins. We'll go feed the ducks." Art paused and cleared his throat. "If that's okay."

"I'm not sure he'll go with you," Emma said in a light tone.

"Come on, little fellow," Art said with a smile. "Let's you and me go see the ducks and feed them." He reached into his pocket and pulled out a package of crackers.

"Ducks," Logan repeated, toddling over to him.

Emma looked on in amazement as her son took the foreman's hand and off they went. "Be careful," she called out lamely.

"Don't worry. Art won't let anything happen to that boy."

Emma shook her head. "I'm amazed at Logan's sudden friendliness to strangers."

"Ready?" Cal asked, reaching a hand down to pull her up. Before she thought, Emma took it, then was sorry. Her pulse spiked as she peered into his eyes, openly seducing her on the spot.

She couldn't continue like this. What kind of woman was she, anyway, to care about a man who wanted to take her child away from her? Stop it! she told herself, feeling her sanity reassert itself. There was no way she would become a casualty of this man.

"I'm ready," she said, turning loose his hand.

A few minutes later Emma and Cal stood in front of the corral fence.

"What do you think?" he asked, peering down at her.

She heard the little-boy eagerness in his voice and didn't want to dash it, so she said, "He's a beauty, all right, though somewhat scary-looking."

"Nah, he's harmless. Hey, you want to see me take him for a spin?"

"So you can show off, huh?" she asked in teasing voice.

Cal grinned with a shrug. "Yeah. I'll admit it."

"Go for it," she said in a slightly rattled tone. She wasn't sure she liked the idea of Cal getting on an untrained horse.

"It's okay," Cal said in a gentle tone, as though reading her mind. "I know what I'm doing."

A few minutes later, Emma watched with her heart lodged in her throat, as Cal was obviously having trouble controlling the animal. The stallion was doing his best to pitch Cal. But he remained doggedly determined to hang on.

It was when Cal glanced over at her that it happened. The horse gave one mighty buck and off Cal went, sailing through the air before landing with a thud on the ground.

At first Emma was too paralyzed with fear to move, even though the horse had retreated to the far end of the corral. Then by some miracle her legs unfroze, and she dashed inside the corral and bent over Cal.

"Cal, Cal," she cried, grasping his shoulders. "Talk to me, for God's sake."

Suddenly his eyes popped open. He then wrapped his arms around her neck, pulled her down, close enough for her to feel his breath. Raw desire beat through her veins, especially when his lips sought hers in a kiss that was wet and hungry.

Emma moaned, wallowing in the euphoria that stampeded through her body. Then that euphoria vanished, and she jerked her mouth off his and scrambled to her feet.

"How could you?" she cried, anger boiling inside her. "How could you?"

Fifteen

Two days after the incident in the corral, Cal was heading out of the house when his cell rang. After seeing the call display, he groaned inwardly. The caller wasn't someone he particularly cared to talk to right now, but he knew he had no choice.

"Hey, Wally, how's it going?"

"When can we expect you, Cal?" His boss-to-be didn't mince words.

Never, he wanted to respond, but of course he didn't. That thought had simply jumped into his mind out of the blue.

"I'm not sure." He scratched his head. "I have something going on here that I can't drop."

"But you are coming, aren't you?"

Cal heard the almost panicked note in Wally Tudor's voice and responded accordingly. "Yes, only not as soon as I'd hoped."

"Man, we need you. In fact, we needed you yesterday."

"Look, you have my word that I'll be there ASAP, but again there's a matter, actually two, that I have to take care of before I leave the country." Cal paused. "If you want to find a replacement—"

"Absolutely not," Wally interrupted. "We want you."

"But you do have someone on standby, right?"

"We do, but again the company hired *you*. Need I say more?"

"No, and I appreciate that. Look, I'll be in touch—say, in about two weeks. Maybe by then I'll have a better handle on things here."

"I'll be expecting your call."

With that, his new boss, the owner of the security company in Venezuela, hung up. For a long moment Cal listened to the irritating dial tone, then switched off his cell phone.

He hated the feeling he was letting someone down, someone to whom he'd given his word, though he hadn't signed a contract. It wasn't that he didn't want to go—he did. He'd been looking forward to this job as head of security for a large oil company ever since he had gotten it. After what he'd been through with the bureau, this would be a gravy job.

With what he had already saved, a two-year stint there would give him financial security, even though he had no plans to retire at this early age. Having reached that conclusion, why was he waffling now? He told himself that didn't make a lick of sense, but it was the truth, nonetheless.

Cal walked to the fridge and grabbed a beer. He'd just come in from mowing part of the pasture and was dog-tired. Yet he was wired. He knew why he couldn't settle down. He also knew why he was having second thoughts about the security job overseas.

Emma. And Logan.

What a freakin' mess this had turned out to be.

When he'd returned to town and learned the shocking fact that he'd fathered a child whom he hadn't known about, much less seen, he'd been knocked for a loop. But he'd rallied, risen to the occasion, and was damn proud of himself. At the same time, his life had taken a life-altering, life-changing course, one he'd never imagined in his wildest dreams.

He was now a father; his existence was no longer just about himself. He had a son to consider. While he wanted to do what was best for his child, he also had to do what was best for himself. In doing that, Logan would be taken care of.

That sounded so easy when in truth it was so *not* easy. Taking the necessary steps to acquaint himself with his child and eventually get custody would've been a joy if he hadn't become involved with Emma.

She was the fly in the ointment. Because he was clearly smitten with her, he'd become hesitant to steamroll over her, take his son and move on with his life. It tore him up to see her pain and vulnerability.

In a few short weeks, Emma had sneaked into his life and set up camp in his heart. By allowing that, he had allowed her to become his downfall. She made him feel guilty, an emotion he abhorred and didn't often have.

He'd made it a point *not* to go that route. If he made a decision and it proved wrong, then he paid the consequences and moved on. His way was to look forward, not backward. Now, however, he didn't know who he was or what he wanted.

Liar, he told himself with brutal frankness. He wanted Emma, his mind betraying him once again, backtracking a week to the day he'd taken a tumble off his stallion and Emma had charged to his side.

The taste of her sweet, sweet lips as they had clung to his had made his insides melt.

In that instant he'd felt something he'd never felt before, and it had nothing to do with sex, though it had taken all the willpower he possessed not to ravish her on the spot. It had everything to do with caring, really caring deeply about someone else.

Most of his life had been about him. He'd never let his guard down enough to let anyone, even Connie, get close to him.

For whatever reason, Emma had managed to do what had heretofore been impossible and that was get inside his soul. It wasn't because she was such a good caregiver to his son either.

Love? *Was that it?*

Nah, Cal assured himself before he hit the panic button. Love was not even a part of the equation. But she'd done something to him, cast some kind of spell over him. As a result, he didn't know quite what to do.

Ah, a thought struck him. He could marry her. That was one way to solve the problem of who got custody of Logan. A hard shudder shot through him. That wasn't about to happen either. Hell, he'd been down that slippery slope once before and wasn't about to do that again.

That short period had been one of the toughest and most miserable times in his life. Out of that nightmare he'd learned he wasn't the marrying kind—certainly not into the same family as Patrick Jenkins.

God forbid!

While Emma was nothing like her sister, or at least overtly, they *were* sisters. Besides, it was ludicrous to think she'd consider marrying him, especially in light of his betrayal. But there was more to it than that. Like him, she was comfortable with her life and saw no reason to change it. Apparently, marriage was not her thing any more than it was his.

She felt betrayed by him and, therefore, despised him. But he also sensed she wanted him with the same fervor he wanted her.

Not going to happen, Webster.

Though Connie had been close to her daddy, she couldn't have cared less about his approval. But to Emma, his approval was obviously important. And the thought of Patrick Jenkins ever accepting him into the family was absurd. His ex father-in-law hadn't liked him from the get-go and still didn't. If the E.R. episode was anything to judge by, he'd do whatever it took to keep Cal out of his family's lives.

So be it. He felt the same way. It wouldn't bother him if he never saw Patrick Jenkins again.

Then there was Emma. The way he felt right now, he was loath to walk away without her. If only he hadn't ever kissed her, hadn't felt the swell of her breasts or her burgeoning nipples under his hand.

Those stolen pleasures had only whetted his appetite for more. Every time Emma pranced her cute butt around, it sent his blood rushing into his groin. The erotic thought of them naked, him on top of her, sucking on a nipple while his shaft thrust inside her wetness…

No!

He couldn't do this anymore. His body wouldn't stand up to the pressure. Even now it was drenched in a cold sweat, wanting her, aching for her. The certainty he could never have her made him want to run for cover, to protect himself from the pain festering inside him.

Emma represented the type of woman Cal had always longed for but knew he never could have. He was much too unsettled for her, too much a renegade for the Emmas of the world.

Socially and economically he could hold his own, even though he wasn't anywhere near Emma's old man when it came to prestige.

When it came to Logan, all that extra crap didn't mean a hill of beans. He had the law on his side, which was his ace in the hole. Or so he hoped. With judges in small towns, one never knew. Judges could be bought. That happened every day, Cal reminded himself. And his ex father-in-law had the power and money to make it happen.

Cal's chest heaved as he struggled for a deep breath, hoping to clear his mind. He peered at his watch, and his lips tightened. He was due at Emma's house in just a few minutes for his scheduled visit with Logan.

A thrill shot through him. He couldn't wait to see his son. And Emma—he couldn't wait to see her, either. The only problem was, she *could* wait to see him.

Cal turned and walked out the door, a pulse hammering in his jaw.

"So what should Mommy put on?"

Logan was in his swing, his eyes on her, wearing that goofy grin.

"Mommy," he mimicked.

"Okay, so you don't care how I look," Emma said, pausing, then leaning over and kissing him on the cheek. "I shouldn't care either," she mumbled under her breath.

She had gotten out of the shower, donned her robe and had put her makeup on. Now, she was trying to decide what to wear for the evening with Cal. After mulling the possibilities over, she had decided on a pair of yellow capri pants, a brown belt and a white cropped shirt.

After all was said and done, she still wanted to impress Cal. While she hated that weakness in her, she had stopped beating up on herself.

But the time would come when the atmosphere would turn hostile again and the down-in-the-trenches fighting between them would start, she reminded herself.

In the last two weeks, when Cal had taken her and Logan to ball games, fishing and swimming, she had learned that he was no pushover. He was going to have his time with his son whether she accompanied them or not.

Whether she liked it or not.

While Cal's attitude certainly rankled, she didn't let on. However, it was taking its toll on her. Much to her shame and disgust, there had been moments when she'd seen the desire in Cal's eyes and she'd wanted to fling herself into his arms and beg him to make love to her.

Then reality would rear its ugly head and again she would ask herself that same question: How could she entertain such thoughts about a man who threatened the very underpinnings of her life?

Cal had already cruelly betrayed her, trying to win her over before coming in for the kill. Still, he wasn't all bad; he seemed genuinely to love Logan. But they both couldn't have him.

For a second, waves of panic washed through Emma, followed by a depth of despair that almost sent her to her knees. God, if this custody matter didn't hurry up and settle, she feared she would lose her mind.

The unknown was tearing her to pieces.

Pushing aside those damaging thoughts, Emma turned to Logan only to find that he'd fallen asleep in the swing. With her heart spilling over with love, she lifted him out, took him to his room, and placed him in his play pen.

He whimpered slightly when she withdrew her arms, then fell back into a deep slumber. She leaned down and gently rubbed his back, all the while blinking back tears. Suddenly her heart was so full of love for this child, it immobilized her.

She couldn't lose him.

She had just walked back into the living room when the doorbell pealed. She frowned. That couldn't be Cal. He wasn't due for another hour. With a puzzled look on her face, she went to the door and opened it.

"I know I'm early."

"That you are," she said in a throaty tone, trying to ward off the siren call of his body at his unexpected appearance. As usual, he looked and smelled good enough to pounce on, dressed in his same attire—worn jeans and T-shirt, that as usual, left nothing to the imagination.

"Emma," he said in a brittle tone, striding across the threshold and closing the door behind him.

Hot, sexual awareness flared to life, taunting and undeniable. Emma's pulse quickened, sending hot blood through her veins. Heat lit Cal's eyes as a groan slipped past his lips.

"Cal."

"What?" he asked, his voice still low and raspy.

"I—"

Wordlessly, he placed his hands around her upper arms,

backed her against the wall, lowered his head and ground his lips onto hers.

With his hot, seeking mouth on hers, rational thought fled. All she could do was cling to him, *taste him,* as wave after wave of emotion pounded her.

"Sweet, sweet," he muttered against her lips.

That was when she felt his hand shove her top up, then fumble with the hook on her bra. Once her breasts were free, he latched onto a nipple and began sucking.

"Oh," she whispered in a cracked voice, circling her arms around his neck, the onslaught so erotically lethal, she lost all sense of self and what she was doing.

All she could think about was absolving the ache that raged between her thighs.

"Oh, baby, baby," he whispered, moving to the other breast where he continued to suck, driving her into a frenzy.

At first she didn't know what penetrated the fog around her brain, but when the noise didn't let up, she realized it was the phone.

Cal removed his lips from her breast and said in a guttural voice, "Let it ring."

She was tempted. Oh, was she ever! She probably would have, too, if Logan's cry hadn't coincided with the obnoxious ring.

Pushing him away, Emma raced to the phone. After managing a quivering hello, she listened; then a cry erupted.

"What's wrong?" Cal demanded, taking the receiver out of her hands and hanging it up.

"It's the nursery. The burglar alarm has gone off." Emma licked her cotton-dry lips in order to continue.

Several beats of shocked silence ensued. Then Cal said, "Get Logan and let's go."

Sixteen

Emma felt numb.

Finally, though, she found her voice and said, "I still can't believe what happened."

"Me neither," Cal responded in a harsh tone. "Damn kids, I'm betting."

Emma spread her hands in a helpless gesture. "But why? Why break in for the sole purpose of vandalizing, of destroying things, just for the fun of it?"

Cal muttered a curse, then said, "Beats the hell out of me. All I know is that I'd like to get my hands on the little creeps who did this." He paused, stretching his lips into a grim line. "I guarantee you they wouldn't do it again."

Now, a couple of hours after the fact, they were back at Emma's, where she had immediately put Logan down for the night. When she returned to the living room, she found Cal in his favorite spot—leaning against the mantel, his features carved in granite.

Emma shivered and blinked back the tears that ached to spill over onto her face.

"It's going to be okay." Cal's voice was low but gentle. "I'll help you put things back together."

Things would never be back together in her life again, she wanted to say. She didn't because she would just be wasting words. To an extent she had chosen this dicey path, and she wasn't referring to vandalism at the nursery, though that certainly contributed to the feelings of despair eroding her soul.

She knew that Cal was also livid at what had taken place. When they had arrived at the shop and walked in, she'd let out a horror-filled gasp. Plants, broken and uprooted, were strewn everywhere. The place looked like a war zone.

"Dammit it to hell," Cal had muttered with disgust, leaving her standing frozen in her tracks while he began assessing the damages.

Finally, she'd gotten hold of herself and was able to function, placing Logan in his swing and checking to see what, if anything, was missing. By the time she'd concluded that nothing had been stolen, the police had arrived.

She hadn't called Patrick, though she'd briefly considered it. Since Cal was with her, that would have been the worst possible scenario. She hadn't wanted to explain why Cal was with her at this time of the evening, visitation privileges having been set for daylight hours. Nor had she wanted to explain why she'd let him take charge of the situation.

At the time that had been a good thing. She'd been so shocked, so taken aback at the disaster facing her, that she'd been glad not to have to deal with it by herself.

The officers hadn't kept them long as Logan was

restless and began whining. They had dusted for finger-prints, but she doubted they would ever find the culprit, or culprits, who were to blame.

Now, as Emma tried to gather her wits about her once again, she felt limp on the inside, as if someone had drained all the resources from her body. Losing plants and other items in the nursery was nothing compared to losing her son.

Items could be replaced; Logan could not. It was that sobering thought that stiffened her spine and gave her the strength to halt the flow of tears. But she couldn't seem to control the shivers that continued to dart through her.

"Hey," Cal said in a soft, but gruff tone, closing the distance between them, stopping just short of touching her. "I know this has been a blow, but again it's something that can be fixed."

"I know that," she said in a halting whisper, sensing she should place some physical distance between them, but she couldn't. His big body, bearing down on her, rendered her immobile. Every nerve in her body clamored for him to touch her. And while that was just plain wrong, she couldn't control her runaway thoughts.

She both hated him and needed him. Right now the need was greater.

As if Cal sensed the emotional battle waging inside her, he reached for her and pulled her against him. At first, she turned rigid in his arms.

"I just want to hold you." His voice was scratchy, as though he'd suddenly come down with a sore throat.

His words were her undoing. With a cry she buried her head in his chest at the same time as his arms locked tightly around her. He simply held her, their hearts beating as one.

Later, she didn't know if it was the feel of his warm breath against her ear and neck or the fact that he was rubbing her back that changed the atmosphere from one of gentle comfort to heady need.

It didn't matter. Nothing mattered except that she was where she wanted to be, doing what she'd longed to do. Her arms tightened around him as his lips claimed hers in deep, fiery kisses that gave her heart wings.

Mumbling something incoherently, he swept her up in his arms, carried her into her bedroom, and placed her in the middle of the bed. Silently and quickly, he removed his clothing and hers.

Standing beside the bed, his eyes trailed over her while her heart beat ninety to nothing. He then placed his hands on either side of her body and balancing himself, leaned over and tongued one nipple, then the other.

"Ohhh," she moaned, feeling as if she'd been zapped with a bolt of electricity, especially when he began sucking those pinks buds until they both were wet and swollen.

"You taste so good." Shifting slightly Cal eased his tongue down the middle of her abdomen, pausing long enough to dip the tip of his tongue in and around her navel.

She squirmed and grasped a handful of his hair as his mouth nuzzled at the apex of her thighs.

Gasping, she dug her fingers deeper in his hair as he inserted one finger and then another into her throbbing wetness.

"Oh, Cal," she whispered, part in agony and part in wonder. No man had ever ventured into that heretofore forbidden territory. Yet she had no desire to stop him. On the contrary, she wanted more, wanted to feel what it was like to have him make love to her *there,* with his lips and tongue, in the most private part of her.

"You're beautiful," Cal said in that same scratchy voice, before making her dream a reality by replacing his fingers with his tongue. Hips bolted as heat flared, sure to scorch her insides. Yet he never balked. His tongue continued to stab her most vulnerable place until moan after moan rent the air.

When Emma thought she couldn't stand another moment of that tender assault, he removed his head, worked his way back to her lips where he kissed her.

"Man, how I want you." Cal's tone was barely recognizable as he pulled back and peered into her eyes.

"And I want you," she whispered, her legs spreading as if they had a mind of their own.

Without taking his hot gaze off her, Cal positioned himself just inside her. Then, one perfect thrust later, he was buried deep and high in her.

"Oh, Cal," she cried, wrapping her legs around his buttocks and clamping down.

"Yes, oh, yes," he ground out before his lips and teeth latched onto a nipple.

Emma cried out, giving in to the pleasures that consumed her body. It was after those thrusts became bolder, longer and stronger that they cried out in unison.

Moments later, Cal collapsed on top of her and they held each other, breathing as one.

Dare she touch him?

Emma's breath hung suspended while the soft glow of a lamp in the corner of the room allowed her access to his naked body. And what a body it was, too.

Perfect.

That was the only way to describe him. While she'd told herself from the onset that he was a magnificent male animal, she'd never had the proof until now. Sprawled next to her without one stitch covering him, he was splayed out in all his glory for her eyes only.

Thank goodness he was sound asleep. Her eyes traveled up and down his body, taking in the mat of hairs on his chest, the broad width of his tanned shoulders and the hard muscles that shaped his stomach. But it was his penis, surrounded by the tangled web of dark hair, that drew her gaze and held it.

The temptation to touch him was growing stronger.

Suddenly his manhood seemed to turn hard. Swiftly her gaze collided with his, a banked-down fire blazing in his eyes.

"I—" Emma's voice shut down. All she could do was continue to stare at him in a wide-eyed stupor, realizing she'd been caught red-handed.

"Like what you see?" His voice was rugged and deep.

Her face suffused with color, though she didn't know why she was embarrassed, especially after their hot passionate lovemaking a few hours before.

Perhaps it was because she'd been caught blatantly staring at him, having never had the pleasure of perusing a man's nude body at will.

"You didn't answer my question."

"Yes," she managed to eke out.

"Would you like to touch me?"

Her breath caught. Oh, would she ever! And more. She'd like to *taste* him.

"It's okay," he said with difficulty. Then smiling, he added, "You can have your way with me."

She knew his humor was aimed at lightening the erotic tension that held them in its grip, but that attempt failed. Nothing could loosen that grip.

"I don't—" She broke off again, licking her lips.

"It's your call," he said in a strained voice.

Deleting from her mind anything but him and how much she wanted him, Emma circled her hand around the long, thick shaft, then lowered her mouth onto the velvet head.

"Oh," he cried out, his hips bolting upward.

Had she hurt him? She lifted her lips and stared at him.

"Please, don't stop," he pleaded. "Don't stop."

Needing no further invitation to do what she ached for, she once again took him into her mouth, sucking and licking until he muttered in a tortured tone, "No more," lifting her up and over him.

Only after she had sunk onto that turgid flesh and begun to ride him did wave after wave of ecstasy wash through her, sending her soaring to new heights. Finally, spent, she rolled off him.

Cal wordlessly nestled her in the crook of his arm, and she closed her eyes.

Fool!

She'd gone and done it now. She had done what she had sworn never to do. Not only had Cal cracked the shell she had built around her heart, he'd knocked it down as though it had been made of cardboard instead of steel.

Now, in the light of day, alone and petrified by her actions last night, she'd been functioning like a robot all morning and afternoon, doing what she had to do—dressing and feeding Logan, taking him to daycare and supervising the nursery cleanup.

Lastly, she'd dealt with Patrick who was not happy that she had waited until this morning to call him about the incident. Her only saving grace had been that her dad didn't suspect Cal had been involved. She aimed to keep it that way.

Ordinarily it was Patrick she leaned on when the going was tough, but not this time. If he even suspected she had been intimate with Cal, his fury would know no boundaries. Besides that, it would severely cripple their relationship. It could even sever it, she told herself with brutal honesty.

One of her father's flaws was his unforgiving nature. If anyone ever crossed him, Patrick never forgave nor forgot. Only Connie had been the exception to that rule. Though it smarted, Emma had come to terms with that brutal fact long ago.

Connie had been the fair-haired princess who could do no wrong. While Emma knew Patrick loved her, she *could* do wrong. She had proven that by having sex with the enemy. At least that would be her father's take on the situation.

He would be dead on target, too.

She had indeed done the unthinkable; she had slept with the enemy.

Oh, God, Emma cried silently, pausing in her pacing to try and make sense of her thoughts. How could she undo the wrong that had been done? She had reached the conclusion that last night's lovemaking had placed her in much too vulnerable a position. Now that she and Cal had made love, would he find a way to use that against her if things got nasty?

"Please, no!" she cried and fell to her knees. That couldn't be the case. She was just playing mind games, *her* mind turning against her. Cal cared for her. But how much?

Another round of panic clawed at Emma. Did he want Logan more, so much more that he would try to use last night to discredit her? Would he do that? Could he do that? More importantly, could she trust him?

Not at this point, she told herself. If he had betrayed her once, he'd do it again. Anger and panic now filled every crevice of her mind and soul. How could she have let her emotions override her better judgment and common sense?

As her face flamed, the details of their evening rose up in vivid detail to torment her. Sexual gymnastics had been the order of the night. No man had ever done to her body what Cal had done.

Looking back, flirting with him had been harmless; even exchanging hot kisses had been okay. But making love in such an all-consuming way went beyond the boundaries she had set for herself.

She had to admit, though it made her sick to her stomach, that she had enjoyed every minute of that hot sexual encounter and just thinking about it set her blood to simmering all over again. She still wanted Cal with the same passion she had last night, which made her think the devil had taken up residence in her soul.

Because of the consequences.

Oftentimes judges frowned on that sort of irresponsible behavior. Because she had fallen so willingly into bed with him, had her vulnerability handed Cal any ammunition he could use against her? And what about her humiliation if it came out in court that she had been so gullible? Last, but not least, what about Patrick's reaction and his embarrassment?

Again, how could she have been so careless, so *stupid,*

as to risk her child's future and safekeeping? Stop it! she told herself. Only she couldn't stop her thoughts any more than she could stop her heart from beating. Anger and panic filled every crevice of her soul to the extent that she needed help, someone who could comfort her with good advice.

Fifteen minutes later she was in Patrick's attorney's office, her heart beating wildly.

"What brings you here, my dear?" Russ Hinson asked, sitting behind his desk. "Especially in such a high snit?"

"First, thanks for seeing me."

"If I hadn't, I would've had to deal with Patrick's wrath."

She sat up straighter. "You didn't tell him I was coming, did you?"

"Of course not." Russ frowned. "What's going on that you obviously can't confide to your father?"

Although she couldn't look him in the eye, Emma did manage to tell him the stupid stunt she had pulled. When she had finished, there was a long silence.

"I screwed·up," she said at last in a flat tone.

"Not because you slept with him."

Her heart swelled with renewed hope, but she still needed more convincing. "But I thought—"

Russ smiled. "Your mind is your own worst enemy. Otherwise, you would've realized that Webster is just as culpable as you, because he's Logan's father."

The tightness in Emma's chest eased, and she felt as though she'd been saved from a fate worse than death— the loss of her son.

"However, you could still lose Logan."

Fear rammed through her, and she stared at him in dis- belief. "I...I don't understand."

"If you'll think about it for a moment, you will. Have Logan and Cal bonded? Let me put it to you another way, is Logan receptive to Cal?"

Emma gave him a puzzled look, then said, "Yes, they have, and yes, he is."

"That's why you could lose your son, *not* because you slept with his father."

Emma sat paralyzed, feeling the bottom drop out of her world.

Seventeen

"Elizabeth, I don't know how to thank you."

Emma's friend sighed. "Don't thank me yet. I may not be able to find what you need."

"I'm not worried," Emma said with more conviction than she felt. "I have faith in you."

"Does Patrick know what you're up to?"

"Absolutely. I discussed my plan with him before I called you."

"I would've thought he might have someone else in mind more capable than me."

"There's none more capable than you, my friend. When it comes to computers, you're the best."

"Okay. I'll do what I can and get back to you."

"Eliz—"

"I know," Elizabeth said, interrupting. "ASAP."

"Actually, it's more urgent than that." Emma's chest suddenly constricted. "I needed the goods yesterday."

"Again, I'll do my best," Elizabeth said in an upbeat voice. "You hang in there, okay?"

That conversation had taken place the day after she'd made love to Cal. After nursing her raw insecurities as long as she could stand it, Emma had resorted to what she saw as a drastic measure. She had contacted her friend and sought her help.

Now, every time Emma thought about what she'd done, her anxiety rose another level. She had been home from work long enough to feed Logan and then play with him before his little eyes drooped with fatigue. Once she put him to bed she showered and slipped into a pair of lounging pj's.

Now, physically and emotionally drained, Emma made her way to the chaise lounge in her bedroom and practically fell onto it.

She'd taken a big step in calling her computer-guru friend and asking her to use her skills to nail Cal, to get some dirt on him, if you will. A feeling of undeniable guilt made Emma wince, which drove her to her feet. She could no longer sit; she was too anxious.

And torn.

If only she could control her fractured emotions, she might get through this latest nightmare without having a breakdown. She had no choice in the matter, she reminded herself. For Logan's sake, she had to remain strong and in control.

So you can beat Cal at his own game.

She still couldn't believe she'd decided to pit herself against him, not when she'd made mad, passionate love to him only a few nights ago. But didn't the shrinks say that there was a fine line between love and hate?

Suddenly her insides froze. *Love?* Where had that come from? Out of left field obviously, she told herself with contempt. She didn't love him. That just wasn't possible, although she had to admit she wanted him. At least she craved his body; every second of their night together flashing before her eyes in vivid detail.

The way he had worshiped her body, and she his, had been like nothing she'd ever experienced. Everywhere his mouth and fingers touched had burned her flesh, sent her into a frenzy. Remembering how he looked naked—

Shallow breath rushed in and out of her lungs, folding her over like a question mark. Oh, God, she had to stop thinking like this. She had to stop wanting him, *aching for him.* She knew such thoughts were her downfall; they made her weak. It was that weakness which could allow Cal to move in for the kill and steal Logan right out from under her.

"Not if we get him first," her father had told her after she'd repeated the conversation she'd had with Russ and Elizabeth.

"I'm aware of that, Dad," she'd said with trepidation. "But this route could also backfire."

Patrick's features were grim. "No, it won't—not as long as you remain staunch in your mission and keep your personal feelings out of it." His tone of voice was also grim and accusing.

She flushed, then said, "Trust me, I've got my head on straight. It's all about keeping my baby and nothing else."

Liar, her conscience screamed in retaliation. It was about that dark side of her, the same dark side that her sister had possessed. She was hooked on Cal and the effect he had on her body.

"Good," Patrick said, jerking her back to reality with a thud. "With that attitude and my pull, we'll sink him."

While that earlier conversation with her father had certainly boosted her hopes, Emma knew that sinking Cal was
no sure thing, especially since she hadn't heard back from
Elizabeth. If her friend struck out, Emma would be in a
world of hurt as she had no plan B.

Biting down on her lip to stop it from trembling, Emma
left her room and headed to the kitchen. Although she
didn't want anything to eat, knowing her stomach would
revolt, she had to try. She couldn't remember the last time
she'd had a real meal.

Once she'd prepared a bowl of pimento cheese from
scratch and slapped it on a piece of bread, she merely
looked at it as if it was something foreign. Finally, with a
grimace, she picked it up and was about to take a bite when
the phone rang, stopping her in midaction.

After she checked the caller ID, her heart upped its
beat. It was Elizabeth.

"Tell me you have something," Emma said without
preamble, clutching the receiver for dear life.

"That I do," Elizabeth responded with the same bluntness.

Hanging onto the enthusiasm she heard in Elizabeth's
voice, Emma sank back into the dining-room chair. "I'm
all ears."

A few minutes later she had yet to eat a morsel of the
sandwich. Her mind was too busy soaking up what her
friend had told her. If Elizabeth was right, then perhaps
she did have the big guns to keep Cal from getting custody
of Logan.

Then why wasn't she dancing a jig?

On the contrary, there was a bitter taste in her mouth,
forcing her to push the food away. It went against every

grain of her moral decency to fight in the trenches. Maybe that could still be avoided. Maybe if she tried another approach, appealed to Cal on his gut level, he would possibly have a change of heart.

Miracles did happen, she reminded herself.

The doorbell pealed, stifling that next thought. Wearing a frown, she went to the door and opened it. Cal stood on the porch and stared at her.

"I couldn't stay away," he said in his hoarse voice that never failed to stir her senses.

Oh, please, not now, not when she was trying to overcome the obsession for him which made her so vulnerable. She closed her eyes for a moment and breathed deeply. When she opened them, his big body hadn't moved an inch.

"I know I shouldn't be here."

All the oxygen in the air dried up. "No...no you shouldn't."

"So you're telling me I can't come in."

Through the haze of need threatening to suck her under, Emma managed to find her voice again. "No... yes. I don't know."

"I just want to talk."

"Are you sure?"

"I'm sure."

Without saying anything, she moved enough that he swept past her into the room. After shutting the door behind her, she leaned against it and looked at him.

"Has something happened?" he asked, his gaze wandering over her, those hot eyes landing on her nipples. Suddenly she felt them poke out to be counted. In fact, she could feel his wet tongue as he lashed across them over and over.

Suddenly Emma fought the urge to fling her arms across her chest, to cover herself. Only it was a little too late for that, she reminded herself cruelly. Not only had he seen her naked, he'd licked and kissed every nook and cranny of her body.

Playing the shrinking violet now would be ludicrous.

"Emma," he rasped again, his gaze darkening as though he could read her mind.

Once again her emotions were betraying her, sending her careening out of control. He smelled so good, so like springtime in the woods mixed with the exhilarating aroma of pure male testosterone.

Soon, she wouldn't be able to pull herself out of the quagmire that was sucking her under, especially after her gaze fell to the bulge in his running shorts.

"Cal, what will it take to make you back off?" she demanded out of desperation, having no clue where that question had originated. It just seemed to fly out of her mouth at will. But it certainly severed the sexual tension that drew them to one another like a magnet.

Cal looked startled. "Ah, so that's what's wrong? You've been thinking about us and Logan."

"First off, there is no 'us.' And second, I've never stopped thinking about my baby."

"Neither have I."

A beat of silence.

"I won't give him up," she said, hearing the crack in her voice.

He shoved a hand through his thick hair, mussing it up. That gesture merely added to his animal magnetism, which she still responded to, even though she was repulsed by her feelings.

"And I can't just walk away either."

"How can you do this to me?"

":Dammit, Emma, hurting you is the last thing I want to do. But Logan is mine. My own flesh and blood, and I want to be a part of his life."

"I have no problem with that," she said, reaching her arms out to him in a pleading gesture. "If only you won't take him away from me."

"Hell, I know how to settle this."

Hope flared inside her. "How?"

"We could get married."

For a moment she was tempted to say yes, thinking of waking up in the mornings and making love to him before they ever got out of bed. Then her sanity kicked in and she felt sick.

"You…you don't mean that," she finally said, her throat pulsating painfully.

His features were pinched with agony. "What if I did?"

"It wouldn't work," she said out of hand. "You don't love me and I don't love you."

"That's not the point," he said tersely. "It would be for Logan, for his good."

"How dare you say that? You're my brother-in-law, for God's sake." She shivered. "That would be almost incestuous."

He looked appalled, then said in a hard, cold tone, "Ex brother-in-law. Just for the record."

"I don't want to fight with you."

"Who's fighting?" he said now in a flippant tone. "We're just having a friendly discussion."

She knew him well enough to know that underneath that calm voice and facade, he was furious. Still, she couldn't back down. She couldn't give up until she'd played her final hand.

"In that case, I'm asking you to drop your bid for custody. I'm certain that's in Logan's best interest."

"I love him, too, Emma." Cal's tone was weary. "You make it a point to forget that."

"That's not true," she flared back. "Besides, you're not prepared to meet his needs." She didn't even pause to breathe, she just went on, words tumbling out of her mouth. "Number one, you haven't been around him enough for him to be comfortable alone with you. Number two, you want to whisk him off to a foreign country and leave him in the care of a nanny. And number three, your past *and* present have the potential to put my baby in danger."

Cal got quiet for a second, then said in a dangerous tone, "What makes you say that?"

Emma didn't so much as balk. "I had you investigated and learned something very interesting."

"And just what was that?" It wasn't so much what he said as the way he said it that sent cold chills up and down her spine. No matter. She wasn't about to back down now. Besides, she'd already dug a deep hole. If she was burying herself, she might as well pull the dirt in on her now as later.

"You were seen two days ago in the company of a woman who's not only a known hooker but a drug dealer as well." There, she'd said it, said what had been festering in her heart since that call from Elizabeth.

Cal's only reaction was to stand a little straighter and scrape a hand across his stubble. "That's a cheap shot and you know it."

Her chin jutted, and she glared at him. "I'll do whatever it takes to keep my child."

"You shouldn't have done that, Emma."

A frisson of fear ran through her. "You left me no choice."

"Oh, you had a choice, only you made the wrong one."

"I'm sticking to what I know."

"And I'm telling you, you don't know squat. I was tying up some loose ends for the bureau, which was done successfully and without confrontation." He bore down on her. "But that no longer matters," he added brutally. "When you had me investigated, you put the final nail in your coffin."

Emma's eyes widened and she backed up. She wasn't afraid of him, though she knew his rage was building. "I don't know what you're talking about."

"Oh, yes, you do. I'm not only going to take you to court, but I'm going to do everything in my power to get my child and exclude you from ever visiting him."

She gasped in horror, his words plunging like a dagger straight in her heart.

"Now, you see how I feel." The cords in his neck stood out. "I'll see you in court."

Eighteen

Emma was inconsolable.

She had cried and paced until she couldn't do either anymore. She couldn't stop, even though she was worn out mentally, emotionally and physically.

Maybe she would *die,* she told herself, pulling up short and actually feeling a ray of hope for the first time in two days. It wasn't unheard of for people to die from a broken heart. She'd actually prefer that fate rather than the one she was living.

My baby is gone.

Cal had indeed put a nail in her coffin. Actually he and the judge had nailed it shut. Once more Judge Rivers had ruled against her. He had given Cal full custody of his son.

"I've taken this matter under careful advisement and have reached this conclusion, though I have to say that like most cases where a child is involved, it was not an easy

decision." Judge Rivers had paused, his eyes pinging
between her and Cal.

During that pause, Emma thought she would jump out
of her skin. She had remembered digging her fingers into
her father's arms until she figured she'd drawn blood.
Only Patrick hadn't so much as flinched; he'd merely sat
still and stone-faced.

"While I know you've been a good parent and guardian,
Ms. Jenkins," he went on, "I—"

"No!" Emma cried out, lunging to her feet. "You can't
give my baby away. You can't!"

Following that outburst, she recalled very little, except
the judge using his gavel to restore order, then barking at
her to sit down.

Looking back on what followed still remained a blur,
possibly because she had blocked it out of her mind in
order to survive. Patrick had taken care of her, had gotten
her home where the nightmare continued. There she had
run head-on into reality when Cal had come for his son.

That moment she did remember.

It was the worse day of her life, and she would never
forget it as long as she lived. Nor would she ever forgive
Cal for taking a whimpering Logan out of her arms and
walking out with him.

"It's not like you won't see him again," Cal had said in
a strained voice, his features gaunt and twisted in agony.
"You will. I promise."

Her dad stepped forward and glared into Cal's face.
"You bastard. The only reason you're still upright is
because you're holding my grandson. Otherwise, I'd—"

"Dad, don't," Emma cried in a broken voice, grabbing
him by the arm.

Cal's mouth worked for a moment while his eyes sought hers. She couldn't dare look at him, so she turned away.

"We'll talk later," he muttered, then took Logan, a small piece of luggage and walked out.

After she relived that gut-wrenching moment, another wail erupted from Emma's lips and she sank to her knees, the pain inside her like a malignancy that knew no mercy. "Oh, God, no. I can't bear not having my baby."

Deep sobs shook her as her body gave way and she lay on the carpet, curling her body into a fetal position.

Why? Why? Why?

That tiny word kept echoing through her brain, along with countless other questions that seemingly had no answers. How could Cal have ripped her baby from her arms? Even though she'd known he had been furious with her for having him investigated, she had thought he would relent in the end.

He hadn't, and she hated him for that. Only she didn't. That was the problem. In spite of the pain, sorrow and humiliation she'd suffered at Cal's hand, she still cared for him. No. She loved him.

It was that love that gave him the power to bring her to her knees.

Another onslaught of tears ravaged Emma's body, forcing her to take long, gulping breaths to keep from choking. But again, maybe she should just go ahead and choke. At least she'd be out of her misery.

Then she remembered the words her daddy had spoken before she'd asked him to go home, letting him know she wanted to be alone. It was a thread of hope that reinstated her sanity and to which she now clung.

"This isn't over, my dear. We'll get our baby back. You can count on it." ~

But when? Her heart cried. She wanted Logan this moment, wanted desperately to hold him, to cuddle him. In the distance she heard the phone ring, but she didn't have the strength, or the desire, to answer it. In fact, she hadn't taken any calls in the past two days. She'd virtually existed in a vacuum, in the dark recesses of her mind.

Food? She couldn't remember when she'd last eaten either. The thought of doing so now made her want to throw up. She had showered and brushed her teeth, but that had been the extent of her activities.

It was as if Logan had died.

Another piece of her heart broke off as a sob wrenched her to the core. She pulled her knees tighter into her stomach, then blissfully fell into a deep sleep.

If only...

He'd been playing that game ever since he'd taken his son and walked out of Emma's house. Cal paused in his pacing and tried to brace himself for another painful jab to his gut.

His breath caught, that jab causing a burning sensation to spread throughout his system, poisoning every nerve ending he had. *Guilt.* That was what this trip down Pity Lane was all about, though he'd tried with every ounce of willpower he possessed not to go there.

Not only was he on Pity Lane, he'd set up housekeeping there.

He couldn't get Emma's face out of his mind—the stark streaks of pain that had marred her lovely face. When she had begged him not to take her baby, he'd been tempted to change his mind, to walk away, to get on the next plane out of the country and never look back.

Only he hadn't. The dirty pool she'd played rose to the forefront of his mind and absolved his conscience.

Now, however, he was miserable, but not more than Emma, he knew. He couldn't imagine the pain she must be suffering. And he was to blame. He winced against another jab of pain. What he needed was a stiff drink. He couldn't indulge, however, because of his responsibility to his son. He had to take care of him, though he'd struggled with that endeavor from the moment he'd brought Logan to his place.

Thank goodness, the little fellow had finally fallen asleep after crying for his mother until he was worn out. Thinking about Logan made him turn his attention to the monitor. After listening intently and hearing nothing out of the ordinary, Cal resumed his pacing, only this time he made his way into the kitchen where he opened the fridge and latched onto a beer.

Just one. What harm could that do? Maybe then he could settle down and form a plan. Ha, he told himself, thrusting his free hand savagely through his hair, then over his bristly cheeks. That was a joke. He had no idea what to do next.

Oh, he could feed his son and change his diaper, but apparently he had no clue how to meet Logan's emotional needs. Dammit, how had things gotten so out of hand? He knew. He'd first duped Emma, and then she had duped him. He should've expected that, but he hadn't. She'd caught him unawares and that was why he'd been so livid, so determined to get even. For so long he'd lived by one rule: if hit, hit back.

In hindsight, he realized how stupid and childish that was. Most of all, he'd lost sight of what was important.

Logan's welfare. Oh, boy, had he ever screwed up there.

While he was examining his soul, he had to face something else—he was in love with Emma. There, he'd finally admitted it. In fact, he loved her so much he'd do whatever it took, pay whatever the price, to make things right between them.

He pulled up short, feeling his heart race.

Could he do it? Could he give up his son? That would be the ultimate sacrifice, the ultimate *gift*. No! he told himself. He'd already paid a high enough price to get him. But if neither he nor Logan could function, then what had he gained? Not one damned thing. Hence, he needed to re-examine his motives.

Needed to look deeper into his soul.

It was at that moment he heard Logan's cry. Shutting down his mind, Cal strode into the bedroom to find the child standing up with tears on his face.

When he saw Cal, he began to cry more. But when Cal lifted him, his wailing stopped. "Were you having a bad dream, buddy?" he asked, pushing Logan's hair off his forehead.

The child's head lobbed onto his shoulder.

Cal frowned, realizing that something was wrong. Logan's face and body were hot. Too hot, which meant he had a fever. Great! Cal told himself. Just great. Now what?

Before he could answer that question, Logan made a burping sound and then lost the contents of his stomach, this time saturating the front of Cal's shirt instead of his face.

Cal's own stomach rebelled before he regained control and went about the task of cleaning Logan up, only to realize the child was becoming more fretful by the second.

"Mr. Wiggly," Logan whimpered, though not very clearly.

At first, Cal didn't know what he was talking about, then he remembered. Mr. Wiggly was Logan's ragged teddy bear that he slept with. Until now, until he felt bad, he apparently hadn't missed it.

Where was it? Cal asked himself, settling Logan on his hip while he searched though the baby's belongings only to come up empty-handed. By this time, Logan was not just crying, he was howling.

"To hell with this," Cal muttered, grabbing the child, and heading to the door.

When he arrived at Emma's, it looked as though no one was home. He didn't see any sign of light or life. Maybe she'd run away from the heartache that he knew dogged her every step.

Still, he stepped onto the porch and rang the doorbell at the same time Logan let out another cry. "Shh, son," he whispered, soothing the child as best he could.

Cal was about to turn around and leave when the door opened. "Emma?" he said through dry lips. Surely not, he told himself, barely recognizing her. In two days she had become a mere shell of her former self—openly wearing the scars of unvarnished pain.

He stood helpless against the guilt that filled every crevice of his soul, unable to utter a word. But that didn't matter. *He* didn't matter.

Emma was all that mattered and she only had eyes for Logan, whose little arms were outstretched while he cried, "Mama, Mama, Mama."

"Oh, my precious, precious baby," she sobbed, reaching out and taking him.

Only after Logan had buried his head in her breasts and she had her head buried in his neck did Cal realize that tears flowed down his face. He didn't bother to wipe them off.

"Sometimes a kid just needs his mommy," Cal said, hearing the catch in his voice as that helpless feeling of a moment ago almost swamped him.

"What…what are you saying?" Emma asked in a croaking voice.

He reeled against the incredible sadness emanating from her and cleared his throat. "That there's more to being a parent than I ever realized."

Emma sucked in her breath, then stammered, "What… do you mean?"

Cal didn't hesitate. "You're his mother, and he needs you."

A cry burst from Emma's lips as she stared at him in wide-eyed amazement. "I don't understand. I—" Her weak voice simply faded into nothingness as though it was no longer possible to speak.

"You're his *mother,* and he needs *you,*" Cal repeated, staring deeply into her eyes. "And *I* need you, too."

"Does that mean—?" Again Emma seemed to have lost the power to speak.

"That I love you? Yes, that's exactly what it means. Furthermore, I want to marry you and make a real home for you and my son."

"Oh, Cal, I love you, too," she cried, "and that's exactly what I want—for us to be a family."

With a cry of his own, Cal reached out and folded both her and Logan in his arms and held onto them as though he'd never let them go. "I love you so much that I can't exist without you any longer."

"Nor I you." Emma reached up, pulled his lips down to hers, and claimed him as her own.

Epilogue

"My heart beats for you."

Emma had to get close to Cal's mouth to hear him since his voice was so weak. She shouldn't be surprised. They had just finished a marathon round of lovemaking, with him ending up on top, riding her hard and deep.

Though they were now side by side, facing each other in dawn's early light, he remained inside her. If she so much as wiggled, experience told her he'd spring back to life. A warmth flooded through her just thinking about that and what would follow.

"Surely you don't still want me," he said in an indulgent tone.

"Oh how easily you read my mind."

Cal chuckled, then gave her a gentle kiss. "Oh but I can read your body so much better."

She smiled and kissed him.

"So how was your night, Mrs. Webster?"

"Oh, I so love it when you take my name in vain," Emma responded with a mischievous grin.

Cal chuckled again before kissing her on the nose. "I so love you, too."

Emma's features turned serious as she peered into her husband's face. Their eyes met and held for a timeless moment. "Are you really my husband?"

He trapped one of her hands and brought the palm to his lips. After laving it with his tongue, which sent chills darting through her, he said, "As of a month ago today, my precious Mrs. Webster."

"You just keep taking my name in vain, and I just keeping loving it."

"I just love you, too."

Emma gave a contented sigh, loving that silly little game they had played ever since they had gotten married. At times, though, she had to pinch herself in order to realize this happiness wasn't just a dream.

When she was locked tightly in Cal's arms as she was now, she knew beyond a doubt that she belonged to him and he to her—and that marrying him had been the best thing that had ever happened to her, despite the fact that her father hadn't spoken to either of them since they had taken their vows.

"You're thinking about your dad." Cal made a plain statement of fact.

"That's twice you've read me like a book."

"Does that bother you?" he asked in a somber tone.

"Of course not, silly."

"I'm sorry about Patrick," Cal said on a somber note. "I know how that grieves you."

She buried a sigh. "I won't deny it hurts, but Dad's the one who made the choice."

"Do you think he regrets it?" Cal asked.

"Possibly," Emma said. "But who knows?" He must've heard the catch in her voice because he pulled her closer for a second and held her tighter. "I keep thinking he'll come to his senses and see what he's giving up, but I don't know. He may never forgive me for marrying you."

"God, I hate that I'm the one who came between the two of you."

"Stop apologizing for that. You aren't the culprit here. Like I said, Daddy chose not to sanction our marriage and to turn his back on me. And Logan."

"I understand why Patrick's upset with you, but for him to shun his grandson is something I can't identify with."

"Me neither," Emma responded in a sad voice. "Maybe time will heal his wounds and his attitude."

They were quiet for a while. Emma was the first to break the silence. "Are you still sure you're not sorry about turning down that overseas job?"

Cal sighed, then kissed her on the nose. "Hey, I've told you, I have no regrets about anything. The security company I'm heading now is just fine."

"I hope you mean that. Just don't forget I offered to go with you."

"I know, my precious, and I appreciate that. But since I have you and Logan, I'm not hankering to go anywhere." This time he nuzzled her nose. "Besides, you have your own business that you still enjoy, despite the crazy act of vandalism that set you back."

She winced thinking about that awful episode, though she'd gotten her just desserts fast. Two teenage boys had been arrested; after some intensive questioning by the police, they had confessed. Both had been placed in a juvenile facility, for which she was grateful.

Once the place had been cleaned up, she'd decided to update it, make some much-needed changes. The biggest change had been to add a "pretties" room, which housed gifts for the home and office. She'd had a ball going to market for that.

More than anything, though, she loved being a wife and mother.

"What's going on inside that pretty head of yours?" Cal asked in a husky tone, reaching out and fondling a nipple.

Heat flared inside her and she moaned. "If you don't stop that, I can't answer."

"Aw, I bet you can do two things at one time."

"Possibly," she teased, then added, "I was thinking about how much I love being a wife and mother. And because I am a mother, those two boys serving time for breaking and entering crossed my mind."

"Our son sure won't turn out like them. We're going to love him so much, he'll think he's the most special person on earth."

"Are you kidding? He already does, especially the way you spoil him."

"Me? Why, I'd never do a thing like that."

She grinned, then gave him a long, wet kiss.

"Mercy me, woman," he whispered. "Feel what you do to me?"

"Oh, I feel you rising to the occasion, all right." She giggled, then wiggled her hips.

For a long stretch of time, their groans were the only sounds in the room. Then the monitor beside the bed came to life.

"Mama. Dada."

They both looked at each with wonder in their eyes before Cal said, "Our child is calling, my precious."

With her heart spilling over with love, Emma reached for his hand. "Thank you for loving me, Cal Webster."

His eyes mirroring hers, he whispered, "I wouldn't have it any other way, Emma Webster."

They leapt out of the bed. He put on his pajama bottoms, and she put on his top. Then, smiling at each other, with their hearts in their eyes, they went, hand in hand, to get their son.

* * * * *

Join Sheri WhiteFeather in The Trueno Brides!

Don't miss the first book in the trilogy:

EXPECTING THUNDER'S BABY

Sheri WhiteFeather
(SD #1742)

Carrie Lipton had given Thunder Trueno her heart. But their marriage fell apart. Years later Thunder was back. A reckless night of passion gave them a second chance for a family, but would their past stand in the way of their future?

On sale August 2006 from Silhouette Desire!

Make sure to read the next installments in this captivating trilogy by Sheri WhiteFeather:

MARRIAGE OF REVENGE,
on sale September 2006

THE MORNING-AFTER PROPOSAL,
on sale October 2006!

Available wherever books are sold, including most bookstores, supermarkets, discount stores and drugstores.

If you enjoyed what you just read,
then we've got an offer you can't resist!

Take 2 bestselling
love stories FREE!

Plus get a FREE surprise gift!

Clip this page and mail it to Silhouette Reader Service™

IN U.S.A.	**IN CANADA**
3010 Walden Ave.	P.O. Box 609
P.O. Box 1867	Fort Erie, Ontario
Buffalo, N.Y. 14240-1867	L2A 5X3

YES! Please send me 2 free Silhouette Desire® novels and my free surprise gift. After receiving them, if I don't wish to receive anymore, I can return the shipping statement marked cancel. If I don't cancel, I will receive 6 brand-new novels every month, before they're available in stores! In the U.S.A., bill me at the bargain price of $3.80 plus 25¢ shipping and handling per book and applicable sales tax, if any*. In Canada, bill me at the bargain price of $4.47 plus 25¢ shipping and handling per book and applicable taxes**. That's the complete price and a savings of at least 10% off the cover prices—what a great deal! I understand that accepting the 2 free books and gift places me under no obligation ever to buy any books. I can always return a shipment and cancel at any time. Even if I never buy another book from Silhouette, the 2 free books and gift are mine to keep forever.

225 SDN DZ9F
326 SDN DZ9G

Name	(PLEASE PRINT)	
Address	Apt.#	
City	State/Prov.	Zip/Postal Code

Not valid to current Silhouette Desire® subscribers.

Want to try two free books from another series?
Call 1-800-873-8635 or visit www.morefreebooks.com.

* Terms and prices subject to change without notice. Sales tax applicable in N.Y.
** Canadian residents will be charged applicable provincial taxes and GST.
  All orders subject to approval. Offer limited to one per household.
  ® are registered trademarks owned and used by the trademark owner and or its licensee.

DES04R   ©2004 Harlequin Enterprises Limited